c Petrovka 38
d Vagankovskoye Cemetery
e Sparrow Hills
f Borisovskiye Prudy Park

MOSCOW

mi. 0   1   2

km. 0   1.6   3.2

n.

Nakhimov
Square

Bay of Sevastopol;
Black Sea Fleet

Inkerman

2 Lenin St.

Chorna R.

SEVASTOPOL

n.

mi. 0   1   2

km. 0   1.6   3.2

INDEPENDENCE SQUARE

ARKADY RENKO IN UKRAINE

MARTIN CRUZ SMITH

Simon & Schuster

NEW YORK   LONDON   TORONTO
SYDNEY   NEW DELHI

Simon & Schuster
1230 Avenue of the Americas
New York, NY 10020

First Simon & Schuster hardcover edition May 2023

SIMON & SCHUSTER and colophon are registered trademarks of
Simon & Schuster, Inc.

For information about special discounts for bulk purchases,
please contact Simon & Schuster Special Sales at 1-866-506-1949
or business@simonandschuster.com.

The Simon & Schuster Speakers Bureau can bring authors to your
live event. For more information or to book an event, contact
the Simon & Schuster Speakers Bureau at 1-866-248-3049
or visit our website at www.simonspeakers.com.

Manufactured in the United States of America

1   3   5   7   9   10   8   6   4   2

Library of Congress Cataloging-in-Publication Data
has been applied for.

ISBN 978-1-9821-8830-6
ISBN 978-1-9821-8832-0 (ebook)

For my dear friend
Andrew Nurnberg

MOSCOW

1

"You know what the two most depressing words in the Russian language are?" Arkady asked.

"How long have I got?"

Victor's voice sounded thick with gravel, which was always a sign that the previous night he hadn't so much fallen off the wagon as plunged from it.

"'Desk job,'" Arkady said. "In a country which clasps tragedy to its breast, nothing is more tragic than a man with a 'desk job.'"

"As always, Investigator, you zero in on the truth."

"Investigator." Arkady sighed. "The only inquiry I've made in the past three months has been into the quality of the coffee here in Petrovka."

Petrovka 38 was the police headquarters where Arkady worked as investigator for the Office of Prosecution, and Victor was his good friend and assistant detective.

"What did you decide?"

"That when the devil came to seduce Margarita in Patriarch Ponds, he stopped off on the way to install vending machines. Come on, Victor, what do you call an investigator who doesn't investigate?"

"A crime," said Victor.

It was, of course, Prosecutor Zurin who had confined Arkady to office duties. He had, over the years, sent Arkady to various extremities of the country on cases: to Kaliningrad, hard up against the Polish border in the west, and to Lake Baikal, halfway to the Far East, across endless rolls of Siberian tundra. Perhaps, Arkady thought, he could complete the compass by going to the far north or the far south. The Northern Fleet in Murmansk was always a hotbed of scandal, and any time spent there would play havoc with Arkady's circadian rhythms to an extent which would please even Zurin. The sun didn't rise for six weeks in the winter and didn't set for six weeks in the summer. Men went mad with monotonous regularity up there, and sometimes Arkady felt he had less far to go than most. As for the south—well, Crimea was Russian again now, and it was very nice at this time of year. Arkady had been there once with his first wife, Zoya, back in the days when every woman on the beach wore the same leopard-print swimsuit because that was the only one on sale that year. As the saying went, the past was another country.

Papers were stacked in ziggurats on Arkady's desk. He picked up a sheet off the tallest one and waved it vaguely in Victor's direction. "Departmental liaison officer. Do you know what that means?"

"That you attend endless meetings where you're neither wanted nor needed."

"Right," said Arkady.

The ziggurat slid and toppled as Arkady put the paper back. A solitary sheet floated gently downwards like a snowflake. Victor stretched out a hand and caught it lightly between thumb and forefinger.

"What's this?" he asked.

"What do you mean?"

"The handwriting is so tiny, it's illegible. I can't read a word of it. Can you read it?"

"Of course. It's my handwriting."

"Go on, then." He handed the paper to Arkady. "Read it to me."

Arkady hesitated.

"I can't read a word of it either," Arkady said.

"You should transcribe it onto the computer while it's still fresh in your mind.

"It's called age, Victor. Everything starts going with age."

2

It was June, warm enough for Arkady to take his jacket off and sling it over his shoulder. As he walked, he kicked up what looked like snow but wasn't. It was *pukh*, fluff from poplar trees, which at this time of year could fall in blizzards. Moscow had hundreds of thousands of poplar trees, the planting of which was blamed on Stalin, or Khrushchev, or both. Piles of *pukh* burned like gunpowder, so street cleaners trained high-pressure hoses on the flakes wherever they gathered. In Arkady's early days as an investigator, he heard the tale of the American ambassador who had such a bad allergic reaction to the stuff that he'd been evacuated to a hospital in Germany. Arkady regarded *pukh* in the same way he regarded Moscow's traffic: as an annoyance so commonplace that acceptance was the path of least resistance.

Zhenya was where Arkady knew he would be, because it

was where he always was, at the chess tables in Gorky Park. Looking like a novitiate monk in his maroon hoodie, Zhenya crouched low over his table and stared at the board with such intensity that Arkady thought the king might give himself up through sheer fright.

Zhenya's opponent was an old man in a flat leather cap, a thick tweed jacket, and a pullover, a man in whose bones the long cold winters clearly lingered even once summer had come. He sat back in his chair, pondered, then slowly moved his piece. Zhenya was a dervish, hands dancing over the pieces, crashing a bishop down here, slapping the chess clock there. Each move was designed to set a trap. The old man's queen was skittish and isolated.

"Mate in five," Zhenya said.

"Let's play it out."

"Why? I check here, your king goes there, check, check, pawn cuts off your flight."

"Let's play it out."

Zhenya shrugged. "Suit yourself."

He made a show of impatience as the old man took his time over each move, until eventually it was done. Zhenya pocketed the two one-hundred-ruble notes tucked under one side of the board. He showed not the slightest trace of embarrassment. This was how he made his living.

"I could have been halfway through my next game by now," Zhenya said.

The old man got to his feet as though uncoiling. "I know."

Arkady stopped his smile just short of a laugh.

Only now did Zhenya even seem to notice that Arkady was

there. He gave a sheepish grin and placed his hand awkwardly on Arkady's shoulder. For Zhenya, this represented unbridled affection. "Hi."

"How have you been? Haven't seen you for a while."

They were father and son, officially if not biologically. Arkady had adopted Zhenya after finding him living in a casino off Three Station's Square, and now they did all the things normal fathers and sons did. They argued their way toward common ground, sighed that the other didn't understand them, and wrangled over money both owed and needed. Zhenya had moved out of Arkady's apartment a few months back.

"I've been here."

"How's Lotte?"

"She's okay."

Arkady knew Zhenya, so he waited.

"Ah," Zhenya said, "things aren't so good."

"Why not?"

"She thinks I'm wasting my time here."

"She's right."

"Don't start."

"Zhenya, you have all the talent in the world, and you're using a fraction of it. Hustling pensioners for a couple of hundred rubles, that's not a job."

"It's a living."

"Not the same thing."

"It is."

"You should study six hours a day, play in real tournaments. If that's what you want to do, and you commit to it, then I'll help you."

"How could you help me? You don't even know basic openings."

"Financially, I mean." Arkady gestured to the tables, listened to the clack of the pieces in the warm air. "The money you win here is cheap tricks, nothing more."

Zhenya flapped a hand as though batting away flies. "How's Tatiana?" he asked.

Arkady took the change in conversation for what it was. "Gone to St. Petersburg."

"For how long?"

"Gone as in gone. She's taken a job there. Correspondent for the *New York Times*."

"But you're still together?"

"No."

"Oh." Seeking the right words was almost a physical effort for Zhenya. "Are you okay?"

Arkady shrugged. "We had some good years."

"Why did she leave? And don't say—"

"For the job."

"—for the job."

Arkady had infinitely more experience than Zhenya did, but sometimes he thought that they both knew next to nothing about women, and while that was forgivable for Zhenya, it wasn't for Arkady.

Tatiana had given a dozen reasons for leaving. Arkady chose one of the more palatable ones.

"She told me I lacked ambition."

"Ha! Then fix yourself before lecturing me."

Arkady was still searching for a reply when a young man came over from a nearby bench. He slouched just the same way

10

Zhenya did, barely picking up his feet as he walked. Arkady supposed he should be thankful that neither of them wore his pants halfway down his ass, a trend which as far as he could make out was still popular long after he thought it would have died out, or maybe it had faded and then come back into fashion again, like dictatorship and war.

"This is Alex," Zhenya said.

Alex was carrying a laptop in one hand. He shook Arkady's hand. "Alex Levin," he said.

"Did you read Meduza this morning?" Alex asked Zhenya. "Putin just sent ten thousand troops and an armada down to Crimea."

"Why?" Zhenya asked.

"To block Ukraine's access to the Black Sea."

"Of course," said Zhenya.

"What's Meduza?" Arkady asked.

"It's where we get all our news. The writers are Ukrainian but reporting out of Latvia," Alex said.

"Where do you get *your* news?" Zhenya asked Arkady.

"Remember my old friend Sergei Obolensky? Tatiana worked for him on the magazine *Now*—or, as Sergei called it, *Now and Then*. His magazine was shut down but I'm still in touch with him and he's been telling me about Zelensky and what he's doing in Ukraine. He's become a real hero." He turned to Alex. "Do you play chess?"

"I play with Zhenya just for fun, not money. I could never beat him."

"Alex is a hacker," Zhenya remarked. Alex looked alarmed. "Oh, don't worry. My father's an investigator, but there's no one less interested in computers."

That at least was true, Arkady conceded. "A hacker?" he said out loud.

"I prefer the term 'computer expert,'" Alex said.

"Who do you hack?"

"I identify weaknesses in a company's online security."

"And charge them for the privilege of fixing them."

"Of course. But better I find those weaknesses than someone else."

"Really?"

"Really. My fees are less and my scruples are greater. You'd be surprised how many people still put more locks on their doors than on their computers. The other day we helped 428 American hospitals."

"'We'?"

"I'm part of a loose collective of computer experts. We divided it up and took a couple of dozen each. Hospitals always pay. Especially American ones. I think of it as my little revenge for the moon landings."

"The moon landings were long before you were born."

"The moon landings never happened."

"You think they faked them?"

"Of course they faked them! Think about it. First satellite in space—Soviet. First dog in space—Soviet. First man, first full twenty-four hours, first woman, first multiple crews, first spacewalk—all Soviet. So how come the Americans suddenly get to the moon first?"

"Because Korolev died, and no one was a genius designer like him."

"No. Because they faked it. Stanley Kubrick filmed it on a soundstage in the desert."

"If you say so."

"It's all online." Alex looked triumphant.

There was no disproving what people had convinced themselves was true. How else had the Soviet Union lasted so long?

"It was the year after *2001* came out, you know? They hardly even bothered to make it subtle. Kubrick loved his coded messages. HAL, the computer in *2001*—you know why he called it that?" Alex didn't even wait for an answer. "Because in English the letters *H*, *A*, and *L* come right before *I*, *B*, and *M*. IBM, see?"

"You know he's kidding you, right?" said Zhenya.

"Right," Arkady said. He waved at Alex and Zhenya and started back through the park with a smile on his face.

As he got closer to his car, he could see that a man was waiting by it, and he didn't need to get much closer before he made out who it was. Fyodor Abakov was unmistakable, even by Moscow standards. He was a bodybuilder, and his chest muscles were now so pronounced that his arms hung away from his body. Everyone called him "Bronson," a nickname which had come from his resemblance to the actor Charles Bronson.

He ran protection rackets all over the city—cafes, restaurants, kiosks, nightclubs—and he had been in and out of jail a dozen times over the years Arkady had known him.

Bronson held out a hand. "I should congratulate you."

"Why?"

"I hear you were fired by that pig Zurin."

"More or less. I work at a desk now."

"Consider it a promotion. Can we talk?"

"Sure."

"I can pay you more than the prosecutor ever did if you'll do a job for me."

"I won't take stolen money."

"Then maybe you'll take pity on an old man and help me out." Bronson looked more pitiable than an outsized gangster had any right to. He took Arkady's silence as assent, at least to make his proposition. "My daughter Karina has disappeared down a rabbit hole, and the assholes I hired to find her haven't gotten anywhere."

Arkady smiled. "You don't want to go to the police?"

"I'd rather stick pins in my eyes."

"I should remind you that I'm still technically a police detective."

"Present company excepted, of course."

"Of course."

Bronson fished in his pocket, brought out a photograph, and handed it to Arkady. Karina had curly light brown hair and an abstracted expression. Arkady had never bought the idea that you could tell a person's main qualities from a photo. People changed and turned to show certain sides at certain times. A snapshot was just that, a temporary pause in time, and misleading didn't begin to cover it.

"Tell me about her," Arkady said.

"She plays the violin."

"She plays the violin?" Arkady was surprised.

"Damn right she plays the violin. In a string quartet. They're very good."

"Does she have a boyfriend?"

"You think I'd know? She doesn't tell me anything. All I

know is that she's been busking in the subways. I have her address, but have I ever been there? Have I met her friends? No. I saw a lot of her when her mother was still alive. I think she's ashamed of me."

"Do you think she was snatched in the subway?"

"Who knows? That's why I need you. These kids have a whole different lifestyle. I have no control. She could be anywhere, but she always has that violin with her. Music is all she really cares about. Music and politics."

Arkady's heart sank at the word "politics." Politics in Russia was for the corrupt, the brave, and the foolish.

"What kind of politics?"

"Some movement called Forum for Democracy. 'Forum' for short."

"Anti-government?"

"Isn't everybody?"

The wind rippled the river into ridges. Arkady blew at a piece of *pukh* hovering close to his face, and it danced away as it fell.

"So," Bronson said. "Will you help me?"

It wasn't that Arkady trusted Bronson, and he certainly didn't admire him. But at least Bronson never pretended to be anything other than what he was. Criminals came in all shapes and sizes, and there were two categories Arkady disliked above all: the small-timers who wheedled and sniveled and blamed the system, and the so-called businessmen who thought that putting on a suit and having a chauffeur drive them to work in an office absolved all previous sins in a baptism of respectability.

Bronson was neither of those. He was a man true to himself and the world, and for that—maybe for that alone—Arkady liked him. Besides, he saw that the man loved his daughter and was distraught.

"I've got to have a completely free hand in this," he said. "You can't interfere, and I don't want anyone to see us together, or I won't be able to find your daughter."

"You're sure I can't pay you?"

"I'll do the same job for you either way, so no."

Bronson clapped a meaty paw across Arkady's shoulder. It felt like being cuffed by a bear. "Thank you."

3

Zhenya was waiting outside Arkady's apartment building when he returned.

"I'm sorry about earlier," he said.

"About Tatiana? That's all right."

"Okay if I come up?"

"Of course."

The apartment was in an old tsarist building with a court-yard. Arkady was always slightly amazed that the developers hadn't yet come for this, as they seemed to be doing on every other street corner in Yakimanka. He could hardly move for signs proclaiming PAINTERS' VILLAGE this and COMPOSERS' VILLAGE that. Entire urban blocks slapped with ersatz history and faux artistry because Gerasimov or Prokofiev had once spent a night there between the wars.

"You've still got your key, right?" he said as they climbed the stairs.

"Yes. But I don't like to use it now that I'm not living here."

"This is your home, Zhenya. You can come whenever you want, and you don't have to ask permission."

Arkady put together a meal of salad with ham, peas, potatoes, eggs, and pickles. Since Arkady didn't want to discuss Tatiana, and Zhenya felt the same about Lotte, they ate in front of the TV in companionable silence. Zhenya didn't chat much unless he was discussing things like chess variations, in which case he could talk for hours.

A game show blared from the screen. Zhenya yelled the answers before the host had even finished asking the questions.

"Ten more minutes of this," Arkady said, "and then I want to watch the news."

"What for?"

"So I know what's going on in the world."

"It's all on your phone. Just look at it there."

"Phones are for talking. TVs are for watching."

"When I'm an adult, the news won't exist."

"You *are* an adult."

Zhenya's eyebrows lifted as he considered this. "Yeah. Anyway. If it's on the TV, it'll just be Putin this, Putin that. Same as usual."

"Yes, but he's news."

"Not when everything he says is a lie."

Arkady turned back to the game show.

★ ★ ★

Karina's apartment was in the north of the city, a few minutes' walk from the All-Russian Exhibition Center. Stalin had chosen this park as ground zero for the glorification of the Soviet Union and its manifest achievements. A person could pass effortlessly from the Armenian pavilion to that of the People's Education, from Estonia to the Central Industrial Zones. Grouped among the pavilions were oversized statues like the famous statue of the worker and kolkhoz woman raising a hammer and sickle together. Nearby, a titanium rocket soared skyward above its own exhaust plume. Arkady could almost bring himself to feel nostalgic.

He fiddled with the lockpicks. They were slippery today, not balancing in his hand the way they usually did.

"Here," Victor said. "Let me."

He took them gently but firmly, like easing a stick from a puppy's mouth, and set to work. It took him less than half a minute.

"It's a handy skill," he said as the door swung open.

Neither of them bothered looking for an alarm box. Alarms in apartment blocks like these were not so much ignored as denied on an existential level. An extendable doorstop leaned against the wall, ready to be wedged hard under the handle from the inside and provide at least some form of resistance against forced entry. It wouldn't deter any but the most opportunistic and lazy criminals, which meant that its success rate would be running at around ninety-eight percent.

The apartment was four rooms small, a living room with a kitchenette on its side wall, a bathroom, and two bedrooms. The first bedroom they looked in belonged to Karina's roommate, name unknown. The room was spare. Sheets of music were neatly stacked beside a music stand. In a collage on the wall, there were pictures of a girl with jet-black hair and light brown eyes, sometimes smiling, sometimes serious, and occasionally challenging.

Karina's bedroom was the better of the two. She at least had a view of the park. Arkady peered at the books on her shelves, flipped through her wardrobe, picked through her drawers. Searching was always an invasion of privacy, justified or not, and he had never lost the feeling of discomfort it gave him.

He could tell everything and nothing about Karina and her roommate. The kitchenette was spotless He took the calendar off the wall. The year was 2021 and the month, September, so it was current. Music rehearsals were marked in red, Forum meetings in green. The next one was tonight. A pair of ultrasonic pest repellents were plugged into sockets. Three cans of pepper spray were neatly lined up in a cupboard. He saw toiletries, perfumes, and jewelry. They should have brought a woman with them to read these runes. A woman would know what should be there but wasn't and what was there but shouldn't be. A woman would be able to tell if Karina had left in a hurry or at leisure. There was no sign of a violin, so presumably Karina had taken that with her. That was something concrete, at least. That and the calendar.

"How much did you say Bronson's paying you?" Victor asked.

"He isn't."

"Then he can't say he hasn't gotten his money's worth."

Arkady took the calendar with him when they left. He felt as though he'd somehow been swindled at the fair.

4

The residents of Patriarch Ponds seemed very put out by the fact that a Forum meeting was being held there. Arkady suspected that this was a good part of the rationale behind the choice of location in the first place. The heads of a dowager and a bald man appeared with cuckoo clock synchronicity at adjacent windows of an apartment building.

"Quiet down!" yelled the dowager.

"I'm calling the police!" the bald man shouted.

There was optimism for you, Arkady thought.

The meeting had attracted a couple of hundred people, spilling out of the cafés and bars which skirted the edge of the pond. There was only one pond now, down from three, but no one had gotten around to changing the name. Arkady saw people sitting on steps eating takeout. It felt like a carnival as much as a political meeting.

"Why are so many people wearing green?" Victor said.

Arkady looked. Victor was right. There were green T-shirts, green scarves, green bandanas and baseball caps. He remembered that the Forum meetings had been marked on Karina's calendar in green ink.

"I do know, but I can't remember." It remained just out of reach. He could sense it floating nearby, something he'd read or something he'd seen.

A cheer went up. A man with an eye patch bound onto a makeshift stage. "*Zelyonka!*" Arkady said suddenly, his mind making a muscular leap at the realization. "Lebedev"—he indicated the man with the eye patch—"had *zelyonka* sprayed into his face by political opponents."

"What's *zelyonka*?" Victor's knowledge of the world was limited. He could remember things that happened decades ago but found himself stumped by the most commonplace and recent events, depending on when, where, and how often he drank.

"It's a brilliant green dye," Arkady said, "maybe a disinfectant; I can't remember. It's impossible to get off once it's on you. Sometimes you can still see traces of it a couple of weeks later. In Lebedev's case, it was mixed with something caustic, so he suffered a chemical burn to one eye and lost most of his sight in that eye. Now they all seem to be wearing green in solidarity."

"Did they ever find out who did it?"

"Unlikely."

Lebedev held up his hands, and the applause gradually died down.

"My friends," he said. There was a slight echo on the microphone. "It's so good to see so many of you here tonight."

"Locusts!" the dowager shouted from her window. "Buzz off, all of you."

"Come and join us, madam." Lebedev rode the swell of laughter. "Be part of the green revolution. Come one, come all. As long as you want change, you will always find a welcome here."

The dowager huffed, but Arkady saw indulgence flit across her face. That was the eye patch doing its work, he thought, transforming Lebedev into a pirate, a rogue, the sexiest of outlaws willing to storm the Kremlin's ramparts. Arkady had no doubt that the attack had been real, but Lebedev had made the most of it. That was why he was a politician, Arkady supposed.

"I have an announcement," Lebedev said. "Tonight, for the first time—I made the final decision only a few hours ago— I tell you all: I'm running for mayor of Moscow."

Another cheer went up, even louder than the first one. Arkady's view was obscured by a forest of arms, hands clapping high above heads or fists punching the air. A couple of thick necks in front of Arkady and Victor were among the few who didn't cheer. Arkady noticed they weren't wearing green either. He nudged Victor and nodded in their direction. Victor made a *What else did you expect?* expression. Of course, the FSB, the Federal Security Service, would be here. They would want people to know that they were here. They could easily have sent younger agents who could blend in better. The FSB always had reasons. The trick was to work out what those reasons were.

"I'll need donations, of course," Lebedev said. "Please spare what you can, even if it's not that much. We all know how awash with money our politics are and how you need to be either an oligarch or in the pocket of one to achieve office. Let's change that. I don't want a million rubles from one person. I want a hundred rubles from ten thousand people: clean money, pure money, money given by people who can barely afford it because they believe in a better future for everyone, not just for themselves."

The roar felt guttural, rising from somewhere deep inside the earth. There was such a longing for men like these, Arkady thought, men who held out the prospect of sunshine after rain, even when that rain fell day after day.

"They'll accuse me of being a Western puppet subverting the regime," Lebedev continued. "They're half-right. If campaigning against corruption is subverting the regime, then count me in, and count me in if demanding a free press subverts the regime."

Arkady remembered Mikhail Kuznetsov, a billionaire who had also gone up against Putin and ended his days dead in Lake Baikal's icy waters. Tatiana had been covering the story, and Arkady never got to the bottom of her relationship with Kuznetsov. "Purely professional," she'd always say. "At least on my part. I knew he liked me, and I used it because that's what journalists do." And he had believed her, most of the time. He had wanted to believe her, and he knew that even a hint of suspicion didn't help him in any way at all. A suspicious man can never have his fears assuaged, not totally. He can only assume that he has yet to find the evidence which will confirm them. Suspicion led to purges if you were a Soviet leader and to madness if you were anyone else. Not that it stopped Arkady, of course.

He dragged himself back to what Lebedev was saying.

Would he have any more success than Kuznetsov had? Would this be even a single paving stone on the road to change? Or was it all just noise and fury?

"Probably run by the Kremlin itself," Victor said.

Arkady had to agree. Lebedev gave a nod to the democratic process and a veneer of respectability without risking any real damage. He had figured out the algorithm from start to finish. It made sense.

"Cynic."

"Realist." Victor nodded his head toward the front again, this time to a few rows in front of the FSB men. "And I think I've found someone you know."

Arkady followed his gaze until he saw Zhenya and his friend Alex.

5

Arkady sought out Zhenya the next day in the park. "Shall we play a game?" he asked.

"For money?"

"Of course for money."

"Okay. Two thousand rubles."

"Two thousand?"

"Special rates for law enforcement personnel." Zhenya enunciated the words clearly as though trying the joke on for size. "I'll let you go first. Five-minute game."

Zhenya didn't offer odds of a piece, even though he could have given up a rook and still be almost certain of winning. For a fun game, perhaps, but for Zhenya there was no such thing. Arkady pushed his pawn forward two squares and punched his clock.

"Let's play the Sicilian. Sharp and counterattacking," Zhenya said.

They played by the book, moving their pieces quickly. Zhenya opted for the Najdorf variation on the fifth move.

"I saw you at the Forum meeting last night," Arkady said.

"Are you keeping tabs on me?"

"Not at all. I didn't even know you were there until Victor pointed you out."

"What were you doing there?"

"Looking for her." Arkady dropped Karina's photo onto the board. It landed askew against one of Zhenya's bishops. Zhenya picked it up, played a move, punched his clock, and only then examined the picture. "You know her?"

"Sure. Her name is Karina Abakova."

"When did you last see her?"

"At the last meeting, I guess."

"Yesterday's?"

"No. The one before that. A couple of weeks ago."

"You know her well?"

"Not really. Alex is sweet on her. He flushes redder than a Soviet flag whenever she's around." Arkady heard the scorn for what it was. "I know her friend better."

"Her friend?"

"Elena. They play in a string quartet together."

Arkady moved a knight to give his queen some air. "Do you have her phone number?"

"No, but I can get it. One of the other Forum guys will have it." He nodded toward the board. "Are you sure you want to do that?"

Arkady hesitated. "Yes, I'm sure."

Zhenya's knight leapt high and took a rook.

"How did you get involved with Forum in the first place?"

"Alex took me."

"He's into politics?"

"I guess."

"You know some FSB spies were there yesterday?"

"Yeah, I saw."

"Be careful."

"I'm sure they've got bigger fish to fry than me."

"They operate on blue whale principles."

"What's that?"

"No plankton too small."

Zhenya glanced at the board. "Mate in four. Don't be like the asshole yesterday and play it out. I wouldn't lie to you about this."

That was true enough, Arkady thought. Zhenya won games with cheap tricks, but tricks weren't lies. Chess was a game of insight. Nothing was hidden. It was all there if only one was good enough to see it.

"Can you ask Elena to meet me here tomorrow?"

"What time?"

"Noon." Arkady stood up and laid a stack of rubles down on the table.

6

Arkady recognized Elena the moment he saw her, and the look she gave him was no less challenging than the one he'd seen in her bedroom.

"I must apologize," Arkady said. "My colleague and I searched your apartment the other day. We were looking for clues that might help us find Karina."

"In that case, congratulations on your professionalism."

"You didn't notice we'd been?"

"No."

"But I took a calendar from the kitchen."

"I thought it had fallen down behind the stove. It sometimes does, and it's hell fishing it out again."

There was a crowd by the chess players today, offering advice and laying bets on their favorite players. Arkady gestured toward the fountain in the distance. "Walk with me?"

"Sure."

"Kyiv?" Arkady said.

"Excuse me?"

"Your accent. I can hear hints of Kyiv."

"Very good. I've lived there since 2014." She paused, waiting for him to make the connection. Again it took him a moment longer than he felt it should have.

"Crimea," he said. "You're originally from Crimea."

"Very good."

"You're a Tatar." It was in her face. Slightly tanned skin, a tilt to the eyes, high cheekbones, and a watchful defiance. Many Crimean Tatars had left the peninsula for Kyiv after the Russian annexation—an invasion or a reclamation, depending on whose side you took.

"Karina's not a Tatar but she's from Crimea too," she said.

"I didn't know." He had never thought to ask Bronson about his family history.

"That's one of the reasons we hit it off. She's sympathetic to our cause, unlike most Russians who live there. No one dares to denounce the invasion. She does."

"And you play in a string quartet together?"

"Yes. She's first violin, I'm second. But for the moment I'm playing first while she's gone."

"Kind of a coincidence."

"What is?"

"You're both from the same place, you play the same instrument, you're fighting for the same thing."

"We became roommates after I met her at Forum."

"And she hasn't told you where she's gone?"

"No."

"Does that worry you?"

"Yes."

"Does she normally take off without telling you?"

"No." Elena sighed. "But I probably shouldn't worry. She knows how to take care of herself."

"Her father doesn't think so."

"Of course he doesn't. He's her father. That doesn't make it less true. She's fearless. Lots of people like to say they are, but most of them don't mean it. She does."

"You and Karina are involved in an anti-government organization. You know that the FSB monitors groups like Forum and sometimes they bring people in for questioning."

"Maybe she's met a man."

"Does she often?"

"Sometimes. They never last long. I don't bother getting to know them. Saves time."

"You don't think this is about a man, do you?"

"No, I don't for some reason."

They reached the fountain. Elena's brown eyes turned a brief hazel as they caught the sun.

"There's a demonstration planned for the weekend," she said. "You should come."

★   ★   ★

Lubyanka. Even now, the name sounded like a gunshot. Once a prison, it was now the headquarters of the FSB. Beyond the yellow brick façade were cells burrowed deep into the city's bedrock, boxes devoid of light and hope. There, prisoners had been tortured and killed first by the NKVD, then the KGB, and now the FSB.

Arkady asked for Marina Makarova, a forensic pathologist he had known for years. He was told she'd be right out. He wasn't asked if he wanted to go up to her office, and if he had been asked, he would have refused. He always kept the main door in sight when he came here.

Marina arrived with a clacking of heels and a pair of air kisses that stopped just short of Arkady's cheeks. "What can I do for my favorite investigator?"

"I'm looking for a Karina Abakova."

"And you think she might be here?"

"It's a possibility. She's a member of Forum."

"Arkady, you know I can't disclose the names of our guests."

"Guests? But you can tell me if you *don't* have someone here."

Marina sighed. "For you, I suppose. Forum, you say?"

"Yes."

"We spend more and more of our time with groups like that. It used to be all Chechens and Ossetians. You knew where you were with them. They'd kill you as soon as look at you. Now it's kids with cell phones who think they're going to change the world."

"It's hardly the same."

"Of course not. That's my point. I never felt I was wasting my time with the Caucasus. But these kids—how long do you think they would have lasted with the Soviets?"

"But now the Kremlin considers them a threat too."

She put her hand on Arkady's arm. "Leave it with me. How's Tatiana?"

"Gone to the Winter Palace and the *Bronze Horseman*."

Marina made no attempt to hide her glee. "Well, you know where I am."

34

★　★　★

Arkady had scarcely arrived back at his desk when Zurin came in. He was wielding a sheaf of papers like a cudgel.

"What use are these to me? Totally illegible." He slapped them down hard on Arkady's desk. Dust motes rose in indignant protest. "Even a child has better handwriting. Renko, you're getting sloppy. Rewrite these forms so I can read them. What's the matter with you, anyway?"

"I'm not sleeping well."

"Why?"

"Don't know why."

"Well, do something about it. See a doctor."

7

It was a sleep-inducing scene. Across the room was an old woman knitting with busy fingers and balls of yarn. A man with a florid nose sat beside her and looked as though he had been dragged in by his ears. He flipped through a medical pamphlet and mumbled about the unfairness of life in general.

This was the Polyclinic, and so far Arkady had been waiting for an hour and a half.

A nurse appeared. "Arkady Renko?"

He got to his feet and followed her. Florid Nose looked personally affronted.

Dr. Pavlova was as plump as a dove, but Arkady had never known her not to be angry; maybe it was the strain of reading nebulous X-ray plates, maybe it was him. He had come to her so often with gunshot wounds, contusions, and broken ribs that she was frustrated by his apparent lack of care when it came to his own body.

"What brings you here?" she asked.

"A leopard snuck into my bedroom the other night."

Dr. Pavlova paused. "And then what?"

She was used to the elliptical nature of his answers.

"Nothing. It disappeared."

"You said that it was a leopard?"

"Maybe an Amur leopard. It had the tufted ears of an Amur and round gray eyes."

"That's pretty exact. He didn't attack you?"

"No."

"They never do. Nightmares scare you and you wake up. It's an interesting phenomenon in that the dreamer generates both his own fright and his own escape. At least, that's the normal pattern."

"It wasn't really a nightmare," Arkady said.

She sighed as if her pupil had failed a simple test. "I know better than you. Have you experienced any headaches?"

"Just the hallucinations. Sometimes I see a cat sitting on my lap while I'm reading a report."

She drummed her fingers on the desk. "I want you to remember three words: 'apple,' 'sailboat,' 'key.'"

"Why?"

"Humor me. Any hearing loss?"

"No."

"Sense of smell?"

"No."

"Anything else?" she asked.

"My handwriting has become illegible."

"In what way?"

"Too small to read."

38

"Have you fallen lately?"

Arkady raised his eyebrows. "Once last week, as a matter of fact."

These were things he hadn't told anyone; not Victor, not Zhenya, certainly not Zurin. The relief of getting them out was a cool bath in a rock pool.

"Now I want you to follow my finger with your eyes to the right, then to the left. Excellent. Once more. Again."

"I could do this all day long."

She raised both her hands so they faced Arkady. "I want you to tap my right hand, then your nose, then my left hand and your nose. And again, three times. Good. Now I'd like to see you walk across the room a couple of times."

He did as he was told and sat down again.

She sighed. "I think you may have Parkinson's disease."

"What? But I don't shake."

"That may come. It may not. Parkinson's presents itself differently for everyone. Are you familiar with this disease?"

"Not really."

"You've lost nerve cells in a part of the brain called the substantia nigra, which produces dopamine, and dopamine controls balance and how you move. That's why I asked if you had fallen. Did you notice that you barely move your right arm when you walk?"

"So?"

"You have what's called a 'stovepipe arm.' Give me your hand."

She held his wrist and put her other hand on his elbow and gently twisted his arm. "When I do this, the arm should move smoothly; instead, it rachets as it moves. The handwriting, lack of depth perception, and hallucinations are all classic signs of Parkinson's."

His world was slipping from under his feet. "Is there a cure?"

"Not yet."

"Will I die of it?"

"You won't die *of* it. You will die with it. You may die because of it."

"What do you mean?"

"If you fall and break your hip, you might not live through the operation. In the later stages of the disease you may find it difficult to move around and die of pneumonia."

"What should I do? Remember 'apple,' 'sailboat,' 'key'?"

"I'm going to make an appointment with a neurologist I want you to see. He'll recommend medications, maybe vitamins. Be aware that medications used to control Parkinson's can cause impulse control disorders: excessive shopping, increased sex drive, compulsive gambling, binge eating. Things like that. Do you feel you may be susceptible to any of those?"

"One or two."

"After you've seen the neurologist, I'd like to see you again in three months."

Arkady didn't move. Dr. Pavlova's expression softened. "I know it feels like a brick wall has just fallen on you. But it'll be years before you're incapacitated, and therapy will help a lot in the meantime. If you are going to get a serious disease, Parkinson's is by no means your worst choice."

"I can look forward to a slow death, you mean."

"Not at all. No slower than the rest of us, at any rate."

Arkady got to his feet. "Well, thank you. I guess I'll see you in three months."

There was a bench outside the clinic. Arkady sat down and closed his eyes. He thought about Tatiana, with whom he had thought he would spend the rest of his life. She was gone and he was just getting used to her absence, and now he had a disease without a cure. He wondered if life was worth living.

There were, he supposed, three ways to deal with this new problem: acceptance, confrontation, and denial. Acceptance was not so much a strategy as an aspiration. It would come in its own time, presumably once he'd exhausted every other option. Confrontation was all well and good, but it would elevate the disease to a station more central and important than Arkady wanted it to be. He had heard too many people talking about their battles with disease, as though triumph were simply a matter of moral fiber and determination. The problem with that was while his body was the battlefield, he wasn't willing to fight.

That left denial. If he pretended that he didn't have it, he could ignore the ways it was affecting his life.

Denial sounded good.

8

The demonstration that Elena had invited him to was at Sparrow Hills, south of the city, and Arkady knew from the moment he arrived that there was going to be trouble. Every protest was a riot in waiting, but this one was a certainty. A motorcycle gang circled the crowd, riding deliberately close to the protesters and revving their engines as they roared away. There were a couple dozen riders at least, all on large, menacing machines painted black or gunmetal gray, and they possessed a genuine, feral wildness, not so much sheepdogs herding a flock as lions toying with their prey.

Arkady knew who they must be even before he saw the logo of a wolf's head on the backs of their leather jackets. The Werewolves were a gang that acted as outriders for the Kremlin. They had fought alongside Russian forces during the invasion of Crimea and the Donbas in 2014 and they regarded it their duty to propagate and influence what they called old-fashioned patriotic values. It was rumored that they received several million rubles a year from the government. Putin himself had even been seen riding a motor trike with them.

A banner fluttered in the wind like a medieval knight's standard, a picture of Putin shaking hands with the Werewolves' leader, Yashin. There were police here, too, but Arkady knew which side they'd be on.

"This is about to kick off." Victor had to shout in Arkady's ear to be heard above the noise of the motorbikes.

Elena was on the edge of the demonstrators, handing out leaflets. Arkady waved. She came over, quickening her pace to dodge between two of the Werewolves.

"Victor, this is Elena," Arkady said.

Victor gave him a knowing look.

Arkady nodded toward the Werewolves. "Have they bothered Forum before?"

"They show up every time we have a demonstration."

The vast wedding cake of Moscow State University loomed high above them. Stalin had built seven skyscrapers in an elaborate combination of Russian Baroque and Gothic styles. This was the tallest. On a normal day, this place was full of students hurrying to and from classes, couples nuzzling each other's necks, and teenagers scissoring, spinning, and fishtailing on Rollerblades.

Elena looked back toward the crowd. "Leonid's about to speak. I'll see you later."

She darted back to the green mass of Leonid's followers. Arkady wanted to shout at them to disperse a little, to fan out and not let themselves get corralled so easily, but perhaps if they did that, they would just make it easier for the Werewolves

44

to target them. There was something to be said for solidarity, especially when it was an illusion.

ANOTHER RUSSIA! proclaimed the placards. CLOSE DOWN THE KREMLIN CIRCUS!

"Putin, resign!" came the chant. "Democracy now! Putin, resign! Democracy now!"

The Werewolves revved their engines louder in response.

Another voice spoke in Arkady's ear. "Looks like we got here just in time." Arkady turned to see Bronson flanked by two young men with hard faces and watchful eyes.

"Renko, meet my sons."

Arkady gave them a nod. "You shouldn't be here," he said to Bronson.

"It's a free country." Bronson laughed uproariously at his own joke and moved on with his sons until they, too, were enveloped by the crowd.

Lebedev appeared, and once more the cheers and the engines tried to drown each other out. A megaphoned voice crackled. "Disperse, or special measures will be used." Arkady looked over at the senior police officer on sight, but he was just standing with his arms folded, watching the crowd. The voice belonged to a Werewolf with hair dangling halfway down his back and a studded leather bracelet around each wrist.

"Go on, all of you. Break it up. Fuck off home."

"Shit," said Victor. "Who let him out of his cage?"

The nearest Werewolf came at them hard and fast, wielding an iron bar above his head with one hand as he rode with the other. Victor, showing astonishing timing, reached up, grabbed the bar, and pulled the rider off his bike. The man hit the ground and clutched his shoulder with a cry of agony.

The bike skidded on its side, sparks flying, until it came to rest against a grassy bank.

Two Werewolves jumped on Victor, punching and kicking him until he fell to the ground. Arkady waded in and got a backhand to the jaw for his trouble. Three large men who turned out to be Bronson and his sons dove into the melee, pulling the Werewolves off Victor.

Suddenly, Bronson pulled out a pistol and pointed it at the Werewolves. "Back off."

Arkady pulled Victor to his feet as the Werewolves stared at Bronson and his sons in disbelief. They turned away. Bronson's sons looked a little disappointed. Arkady thought of apples falling from trees.

"Thanks," he said. Bronson gave a little bow. Arkady turned to Victor. "You okay?"

"Couldn't be better."

The police were finally getting involved, wading into the protesters and throwing them around. Arkady saw Lebedev being hurried away.

"Where's your girlfriend?" Victor said.

"Not my girlfriend." Arkady scanned the crowd and saw Elena marshaling protesters away from the scene. She caught his eye and made a face: *See, this is the kind of stuff we have to put up with.* The Werewolves, evidently satisfied that the protest was breaking up, formed a perimeter with a gap on one side through which demonstrators could leave the area. They could hardly have made it more obvious that they were working with the police if they'd tried.

Arkady waited for Elena to emerge. Zhenya and Alex were with her.

"You all right?" Arkady asked.

Zhenya shrugged to cover his fear. Arkady's cell phone rang. "Hello?"

"Arkady, it's Marina. Had to do my digging on a weekend when the walls don't have so many ears. Anyway, no sign of your Karina here."

"You're sure?"

"Sure, I'm sure."

"Thanks. I owe you one."

"You do."

Arkady ended the call. "Wherever Karina is, it's not the Lubyanka."

"I can hack their databases," Alex said.

"I trust my source. If she says Karina's not there, Karina's not there."

"Might do it anyway."

"Not on my account." Arkady gave Alex what he hoped was a suitably hard stare and gestured back toward the Werewolves. "Those guys are just the tip of the iceberg. Squirreling around on FSB databases will get you killed."

"They won't even know I've been there."

"Alex, I might not understand the first thing about computers, but even I know that if you're looking for a government that can mount any cyberattack they want, you only have two choices. One is Beijing. The other is just over there." He nodded toward the river and central Moscow beyond. "They'll know you've been there, they'll know who you are, and when I next ask who's in FSB custody, they'll be able to give me chapter and verse on your life story."

"He's got a point," Zhenya said.

47

9

Arbatskaya metro station at half past eight in the morning was a high school science problem in motion. Commuters hurried along passageways in a hundred different directions at once, all staring at their cell phones and yet somehow managed not to collide with each other. How?

Arkady and Elena stood at a subterranean intersection, upturned lamps glowing softly along the sweep of the ceiling above them. They handed out flyers to anyone who would take them. HAVE YOU SEEN THIS WOMAN? There was a picture of Karina and a number to call. No offer of a reward, though anyone who knew anything concrete would certainly ask for one.

"Tell me again how often you busk here," Arkady said.

"Once a week, on average. Sometimes more, sometimes less. It all depends on how many performances we have. Real performances, I mean."

"Paid ones?"

"Of course. How else can a musician make money?"

"How much do you make?"

"For a performance or a couple of hours down here?"

"Either."

"For the concerts, we make what the venue is prepared to pay. Some days are good, others are terrible. Some places pay well, others don't. We haggle a price and either take it or leave it. Down here, there's no haggling. If you add up what we earn by the hour, I'd say we're paid less but surprisingly well, considering we're underground. Usually, we're paid in loose change, but people are sympathetic to young musicians and now and then will throw in a twenty.

"I presume you're good."

"Yes. Not Moscow Symphony Orchestra good, but I hope more than good enough."

"In a sane world, good musicians wouldn't need to supplement their income busking for kopecks."

"Yes, but sadly, we don't live in a sane or fair world."

They stayed until eleven, when the morning rush had thinned and the tourists began to emerge. Sometimes, Elena explained, it was better to busk when there were fewer people around, counterintuitive though that might sound. While office workers pressed for time never slowed to appreciate the music, a man in no particular hurry might slow his pace, enjoy her skill, fish in his pocket, and give her what he could spare.

No one knew what had happened to Karina. That was the flip side of busking. Few people would recognize a musician outside their professional setting. The few who did stop did so only because Elena was too pretty and too well dressed to be

50

busking for money and they sensed scandal or bad luck. As for Arkady's investigation, this was a total waste of time.

Not that he minded. He got to spend time with Elena. It was easy, but then again it often was to start with, when conversation with somebody new was an interesting distraction. People often said that the best way to get over someone was to get under someone else, but Arkady had never quite believed that. Tatiana was still there, not all the time—not when he was fighting off motorcycle thugs or playing chess and arguing with Zhenya—but in the small hours when he couldn't sleep, she was there.

10

Leonid Lebedev had taken over part of the old Red October Chocolate Factory for his birthday party. Photographs of happy guests were up on Instagram almost before they'd been taken. Waitresses in white blouses and black skirts glided silently bearing trays of canapés. Barmen with manicured beards decanted cocktails. Arkady wondered if there was ever a time when he could have felt comfortable in a setting like this. Doubtful.

On the far wall, a giant screen was playing Lebedev's latest video. He had obtained secret copies of plans for one of Putin's estates, a vast pleasure dome in Krasnodar Krai. Figures flashed up over screenshots and computer renderings. It had taken one hundred billion rubles to construct, and the property was forty times the size of Monaco. It was an underground ice palace with two helipads, a church, an amphitheater, a vineyard, an oyster farm. Long stretches of private beach.

Lebedev appeared next to Arkady. "It's like a separate state," he said. "It's where he will flee when we depose him."

He didn't bother to introduce himself. Up close, Arkady saw that the eye patch had gold stitching.

"Elena tells me you're looking for Karina Abakova."

"That's right."

"I've been worried about her."

"What does she do for Forum?"

"She's one of our best organizers. Elena is, too, of course. And news media. Karina's brilliant at getting press interest, and not just from the usual." He gestured toward a small group in the corner. "*Washington Post*, *Die Welt*, *Le Figaro*, the *Times* of London."

"The no-votes press."

Lebedev laughed. "Yes. But that's a very literal way of looking at it. It's not just votes I'm after. It's legitimacy here and abroad I want. Those reporters write about me, my name gets known, my profile becomes higher, and money flows in. Pressure is applied through all the usual channels. It's not enough simply to oppose. One has to offer oneself as a credible alternative."

"And we Russians have always cared about what the outside world thinks."

"I know you're being sarcastic, but I think Russians do care."

No one was better than a Russian at having a superiority complex and an inferiority complex at the same time. Stalin had alternately lorded it over and glowered at Churchill and Roosevelt during the wartime conferences. And men like Lebedev always had half an eye on the West. Most Russian politicians ended up loathed, diminished, and ostracized at home, but the right kind could always find themselves lionized in London, Washington, or Paris.

Lebedev smiled at someone over Arkady's shoulder. "Anyway, Investigator, enjoy the party. Let me know if I can be of any help. We always have people who stop coming to meetings, but rarely when they're as central to our organization as Karina is."

"How many people have stopped coming?"

"Recently? A dozen, maybe."

"Can you give me their names?"

★　★　★

Arkady and Victor split the dozen names between them the next morning and called each person in turn. By the time they'd finished, they had found four who were disillusioned with Forum, three who had been too intimidated by the Werewolves at previous rallies, a married man and woman who had moved back to Nizhny Novgorod after their work contract in Moscow had come to an end, one who was in jail for shoplifting, one who told them that he had never helped the police and wasn't about to start now, and one who admitted that he had only gone to the meetings to get laid and had found himself disappointed in that regard.

Zurin stopped by.

"Have you seen a doctor?" he asked.

"You could say that."

"Good." That was all Zurin ever wanted: to reduce the number of problems he had without really caring about the outcome. "Now I hear you've been sticking your neck into politics."

"All life is politics."

"Don't get smart."

"Okay. How have I been sticking my neck into politics?"

"You've been seen at Forum meetings. Meetings, plural."

"You are well-informed."

"It's my job to be well-informed. Remember who I work for."

"I'm unlikely to forget. Are you having me followed?"

"I wouldn't waste the manpower. What were you doing there?"

"I'm trying to find a woman who's disappeared."

"What woman?"

"It's a private case."

"The Abakova woman, I presume." Zurin accepted Arkady's impressed nod as his due. "If you're working for that old crook Bronson, I can have you arrested."

"I'm not working for him. He's not paying me."

"Then why are you trying to find his daughter?"

"The goodness of my heart, probably."

Zurin shook his head, bewildered.

11

He could justify almost any amount of time spent with Elena as being part of his inquiry into Karina's disappearance. Even if Elena didn't know where Karina had gone, she knew people who knew Karina, and one of them might give Arkady the clue he needed. If there was one thing he had learned over the years, it was that information rarely came neatly packaged. The road to the truth was less a winding one than a maze where all the walls were high and the end invisible.

The quartet was rehearsing Myaskovsky's opus 33. Arkady sat three rows back in the audience seats and watched Elena as she played. She had her eyes closed half the time yet was still able to take her cues.

When they finished, she came over to him with the rest of the quartet.

"Lydia, I want you to meet my friend Arkady." Lydia was the earnest woman with round eyeglasses who had played violin alongside her. "She's playing with us while Karina's away, but she doesn't know her. Misha and Yermolai do, though."

Misha played the viola and looked eager to help. Yermolai was the cellist and bristled slightly.

"Karina gave no indication that she might be going away?" Arkady asked.

They shook their heads.

"No hint as to where she might have gone?"

They shook their heads again.

"No contact from her?"

"Not since the last rehearsal," Misha said.

"Misha's better friends with her than I am," Yermolai said. "It's very selfish of her to go away. We've spent months rehearsing together."

Elena put a hand on Lydia's shoulder. "Lydia is doing a great job in the meantime."

"It's not the same," Yermolai sniffed.

As they walked outside Arkady said, "Yermolai was kind of hard on Lydia."

"You're right."

"Why is that?"

"The strength of a string quartet is how successfully they can musically converse with each other. Everyone looks to the first violinist, but Lydia has been having trouble getting Yermolai on board. Yermolai has started giving us our cues. He instinctively gets the tempo and makes us play better. He's an excellent cellist. Still, it's not an ideal situation. We need Karina back."

"Well, the piece you were playing seemed beautiful to me."

"Myaskovsky was a favorite of Stalin's, you know, like Stravinsky. Just goes to show."

"Just goes to show what?"

"One shouldn't judge music on the basis of politics." She looked at him. "Speaking of Stalin's favorites, I bet you're a Shostakovich man, aren't you?"

"How did you know?"

"Outer conformity masks inner rebellion. That's you."

A flake of *pukh* landed on her tongue as she was speaking. She spat it out. "Summer snow. The only thing I hate more than winter snow."

Arkady reached out to catch a flake on his hand. "Then you must hate all of Russia all year long. How do you feel about Russian people?"

"It's only the long-suffering ones I can't stand. Are you one of those?"

"Why do you ask?"

She laughed back as she went into the subway, "It's all over you."

★ ★ ★

Zhenya was right: TV news was full of Putin and devoid of anything else. On the internet you could, at least sometimes, find real news if you knew where to look. It was the last bulwark against the Kremlin's efforts to drown out what was really going on. At least the Soviets had been honest about their repression, which was to say they had been so dishonest as to have been totally transparent. Newspaper reporters who dared tell the truth were fired and some were killed. Arkady remembered the old joke about the two main newspapers, *Pravda* (*Truth*) and *Izvestia* (*News*): there was no truth in *Pravda* and no news in *Izvestia*.

He was just about to turn in when Elena rang.

"Can you come over?" She spoke fast, her voice high and cracking.

"What happened?"

"I think I was followed home."

"Why do you think that?"

"Because they're still sitting in a car across the street."

"'They'?"

"Yes. Two men."

"I'll be right there."

It took him longer than he expected. Even at eleven o'clock, Moscow's streets were still alive and the traffic still atrocious. He parked outside Elena's apartment and immediately saw the car she meant: a dark Volvo, boxy and forgettable, and both front seats filled by men in cheap suits. No license plate. They may as well have painted "FSB" on the side.

Arkady got out of his car and walked across to the Volvo. It was foolish, taking on the FSB so openly, but since they saw him arrive, and since they probably already knew who he was, he didn't have much to lose. He leaned in at the driver's window and smelled salami and beer.

"Can I help you?" Arkady said.

"What are you doing out here, Renko, looking for trade?"

The passenger laughed, or rather snorted. The driver started the car and, without looking, pulled out, forcing Arkady to quickly step back. He watched until the Volvo's taillights had disappeared before walking back across the road and ringing Elena's buzzer.

"It's me," he said over the intercom. "They've gone."

"I was watching." She buzzed him in.

She hugged him briefly but fiercely as he entered the apartment.

"Welcome to my place, for the second time," she said with a smile. "Can I get you anything?"

"Thank you, no. Tell me what happened."

"I took the metro back after saying good-bye to you. It's only a five-minute walk from the station to here, but I realized there was a car following me."

"How?"

"They were driving really slowly close to the curb."

Arkady pointed at her violin case in the corner. "You're pretty easy to identify."

"I guess."

"Has this ever happened before?"

"Not that I've noticed."

That was the problem, Arkady thought. The FSB were more than capable of following someone without being noticed, especially when they were following an ordinary civilian. Elena had noticed only because they had meant her to notice, just as the FSB goons in Patriarch Ponds had made no secret of who they were. Oddly enough, that reassured Arkady. If they had been planning something nefarious, they would have been a lot more careful.

"I think at this stage they're just trying to intimidate you," he said.

"They're succeeding."

"Take different routes when you can. Walk to the next station along the line rather than this one and at the other end get out one stop early. Maybe put your violin case inside a bag." He paused. "What exactly is it that you do for Forum?"

"I consult with Leonid on messaging and help set up meetings."

"So you're pretty invaluable to the organization?"

"No, Karina is really much more important to the organization. Leonid used to run it by himself, but once his followers multiplied, he asked for volunteers."

"I met another volunteer that you know: Alex Levin."

"Oh, yes, he's a little goofy, but I like him."

"Why do you say 'goofy'?"

"He always wears a hoodie and he doesn't walk, he shuffles. When he isn't working, he has his nose in a book. I think he's shy."

Arkady was glad Alex couldn't hear all this.

"How do know him?" she asked.

"He's my son's friend. They play chess together over in Gorky Park."

Now Elena was embarrassed. "He's a great worker," she said lamely.

Arkady moved towards the door. "Remember to take different routes home."

"Yes. Thanks for coming over so quickly. Just answer me one thing."

"What?"

"Are you really long-suffering?"

He smiled. "Actually, I'm suffering less now."

As he left the building, his phone buzzed. For a moment,

he thought it might be Elena asking him to come back up, but the text was from a number he didn't recognize.

Can we meet tomorrow, please?

Arkady's handwriting might not be legible, but he could type a reply.

Who is this?
Alex
Do you want to meet?
Same place we first met 10 am
What's this about?

There was a hiatus of maybe half a minute, and then three pictures came through.

They were black-and-white, low-resolution, and even Arkady recognized them as having been taken from the internet. Nikolai Gogol, Leo Tolstoy, and Anton Chekhov.

What do those mean? he typed, but there was no answer.

12

Arkady was half-asleep, held in the perfect but unsustainable equilibrium between wanting to stay in bed and needing to get up, when the phone rang. He rolled over, saw Zurin's name on the screen, and groaned. The only thing worse than answering was not answering.

"Renko," Arkady said.

"Get yourself to Gorky Park."

Arkady was about to say he was going there later anyway, but even through his grogginess he remembered that the less he told Zurin about his search for Karina, the better.

"Why? What's happened?"

"A young man's been found dead there. At the chess tables."

Arkady tried Zhenya five times without success as he drove to the park, somehow managing to steer and sound the horn simultaneously with his one free hand until he realized that hurrying was futile. The dead man—could be Zhenya, could be Alex, could be neither—wasn't going to be any more or less dead, and the last thing Arkady needed was to get in an accident.

Alex was the one who had texted him last night and sent a cryptic message, but that might not mean anything. Zhenya and Alex were close, so Alex could well have shared anything he'd found with Zhenya. And if someone did want to warn Arkady off, then how better than getting to Zhenya? Zurin had already shown his willingness to use Arkady's love for Zhenya as leverage against him. He had held Zhenya under house arrest in Moscow, effectively a hostage, in order to make Arkady, who was in Siberia, do something he didn't want to do. Arkady knew he'd never forgive himself if harm came to Zhenya on his account.

Forensics were already on site when Arkady arrived. He searched for Zhenya and finally saw him among a crowd of people gathered around the crime scene. Zhenya was crying. The body must belong to Alex. Arkady elbowed his way through the crowd, reached Zhenya, and put his arms around him.

"He never hurt anyone," Zhenya said.

"I'll find out what happened."

Arkady showed his ID to a uniformed officer and ducked under the tape. Victor, looking crumpled to the point of shapelessness, was standing by Alex's body.

"You look like you haven't slept all night," Arkady said.

"Nothing like a corpse to sober you up." He rubbed his hair and nodded toward Alex. "Poor bastard."

Arkady crouched down. Alex was lying on his back, and the

top half of his head was a mass of blood, tissue, and bone. All intellectual curiosity crushed.

"Exit wound," Victor said. "Shot in the back of the head. Point thirty-three bullet, probably."

Shot in the back of the head could mean a surprise attack or an execution.

"Then how come he's on his back? He'd naturally have fallen forward."

Victor pointed to Alex's blue jeans. The white linings of his pockets lolled out like tongues. Someone had rolled him over after shooting him and gone through his pockets. "Phone, wallet, keys, all gone," Victor said.

"Anyone see what happened?"

"We're asking around. But it was early. The chess tables don't start filling up till nine or ten."

"Silencer?"

"Presumably." Even in Moscow, gunshots tended to attract attention.

"Okay." Arkady nodded at the nearest forensics officer. "Thank you."

He left the cordoned-off area from the other side and found Zhenya. They walked out of the park in silence.

Alex had asked to meet Arkady here and had been killed before he could do so. He had sent pictures of Gogol, Tolstoy, and Chekhov; something cryptic, no doubt, something hidden in their writings. It had been a long time since Arkady had studied them, but like most Russians he knew enough about them to know that they were preoccupied with the meaning of everyday life: the hopelessness, the comedy and the tragedy of it. And what was true then in the nineteenth century was still true now.

Alex with his hoodie and his laptop and his conspiracy the-
ories. A boy who had played at being a man and who'd been
denied the chance ever to fill that role for real. Alex with his ad-
olescent crush on Karina and his ransomware hacks, so adept
in a virtual world and so inept in the real one.

Arkady forced himself to focus, to listen to the sounds
of the park and the city—the birdsong, the traffic, the heavy
breathing and rhythmic footfalls of joggers as they ran past.
It took a few moments, but gradually he felt his mind slowing
and thoughts forming coherently again.

And that's when he saw it: a geometrically neat slice
through a carpet of *pukh*. He stopped to point it out to Zhenya.
The track of a motorcycle tire.

★ ★ ★

"What did you discover?" Zurin asked.

"Shot in the back of the head. Motorcycle tire tracks
nearby."

"Werewolves?"

"You tell me."

"I don't like your tone, Renko."

"And I don't like seeing kids get killed."

"Then do something about it."

"You want me to investigate it?"

"Can you think of anyone better?"

It was a poisoned chalice, of course. Zurin wouldn't have
given Arkady the responsibility of finding Alex's killer if he
thought Arkady could uncover anything damaging, which in
turn meant that whoever had killed Alex was sufficiently well

protected not to need to worry about Arkady's investigations. Arkady would either draw a blank or be presented with a convenient confession from someone entirely innocent, and either way Zurin could say that he'd put one of his best and most incorruptible men on the case and that if anybody could find the truth, then it was Investigator Renko.

Arkady could refuse, of course. But what good would it do? Turning it down would just mean that Zurin would assign one of his yes-men to the job and then the murder would never be solved. At least Arkady could go through the motions. Besides, he owed it to Alex to do it himself and he could now investigate Karina's disappearance officially as part of this case. And it would get him out of the office.

★   ★   ★

Long ago, at the start of his career, Arkady had regarded the mortuary as a hell, a diabolical synthesis of biology and chemistry: rotting, bloodied corpses up against substances designed to mask their smell and halt their putrefaction. No place for the living. Now, hundreds of corpses later, he went in as easily and carelessly as he would a coffee shop.

Alex's body lay on a slab. He was in the same position as when Arkady had seen him in Gorky Park, except for the fact that now he was naked with the outsize Y of the mortician's incision carved into his chest.

The mortician looked barely old enough to be out of school. He turned Alex's corpse over. Arkady saw hair matted around a hole of blood and bone. A particularly undignified way to die, Arkady thought, and hoped that whoever it was had taken Alex by surprise. An execution, knowing he was going to die, would have been an order of terror altogether too much for someone like Alex. Far better never to know that it was going to happen.

"The bullet's over there." The mortician indicated a kidney tray on the side. The shell, old and discolored, rattled against the sides when Arkady picked the tray up. An old .33 rifle shell, by the look of it. As long as the gun was well maintained and reliable, an old weapon was just as good as a new one, and there would be thousands in Moscow alone. It was the ballistics equivalent of driving a gray Lada in communist times: the default choice, so commonplace as to be entirely unremarkable.

The mortician was elbow-deep in viscera when Arkady left. Zhenya was waiting for Arkady outside.

"You could have come in, you know," Arkady said.

"Rather not."

"You want to stay tonight?"

"Okay."

Zhenya was silent as they drove back to the apartment. Arkady had read somewhere that people who were reluctant to discuss things often liked to talk when in a car because they didn't have to face the person they were talking to and because the journey itself could provide a distraction. That theory didn't work for Zhenya, at least not right now. But Arkady was grateful that Zhenya had sought him out.

Bronson was parked in front of Arkady's apartment building. He got out of his car the moment he saw Arkady arrive.

"Hey! You weren't going to tell me about this other kid that got killed?"

"You shouldn't be here."

"Answer my question."

"We're looking at the connection between him and your daughter."

"You think I'm a fool? The connection was Forum, and you know it." Bronson turned to Zhenya. "Who are you?"

"My name is Zhenya."

"I mean, who are you? Are you Renko's son? Friend? Bodyguard?"

"Bodyguard?" Arkady asked.

"I've seen less likely ones, trust me."

"I'm his son," Zhenya said.

"Okay. So, Arkady, is your son the next to get killed?"

"No, and you and I shouldn't be seen together, remember?"

He guided Zhenya into the building.

★ ★ ★

Elena came by later with Leonid Lebedev. Her eyes were puffy and red, and she shivered slightly when she sat. Lebedev made all the right noises of shock and regret, but Arkady could detect the slight edge of performance. A good performance, sure, and by no means totally fake, but a performance nonetheless.

"We should stop the meetings," Elena said. "At least for a while."

"Why?" Lebedev said.

"*Why?* Why do you think? Alex is dead. Karina's missing. I had a pair of goons follow me home. Putin's own Hells Angels beat us up whenever we have a demonstration."

"That's why we need to ramp it up."

"Tell me you're joking."

"Tell *me* you're not so naïve. We're a threat to them, can't you see? They do all these things because they're scared of us. If we back away now, even for a moment, they'll know that we're scared of them too. We need to organize another rally." Arkady knew some version of these lines would appear in Lebedev's next speech.

13

Gogol, Tolstoy, Chekhov. Gogol and Tolstoy in particular had been masters of *ostranenie*, presenting common things in an unfamiliar way in order to wake the audience up and make them see the world with a fresh perspective. Gogol had written books about a nose and an overcoat. Tolstoy had used a horse as a narrator.

Gogol had made a total hash of his job at the University of St. Petersburg, missing most of the lectures he was supposed to give, muttering unintelligibly on the odd occasion he did make it. He'd have fit right in at Zurin's office, Arkady thought.

Tolstoy fought in the Crimean War, including the eleven-month-long siege of Sevastopol. He said that the state ensured that the wicked dominated, that criminals were far less dangerous than a well-organized government, and that governments were essentially violent forces held together by intimidation, corruption, and public indoctrination. Arkady figured that little if anything had changed.

"Remove everything that has no relevance to the story," Chekhov said. "Every element in a narrative should be both necessary and irreplaceable. If you say in the first chapter that there is a rifle hanging on the wall, in the second or third chapter it absolutely must go off. If it's not going to be fired, it shouldn't be hanging there."

Even an old .33 rifle? And how much easier would Arkady's job be if he knew that everything he came across on a case had relevance to the crime?

★   ★   ★

The Werewolves met for a weekly ride every Sunday morning at Sparrow Hills. Perhaps that was why they had been so aggressive at the Forum demonstration the other day, Arkady thought. They regarded the area as somehow their turf and not to be trespassed on, let alone by a group of whiny liberal idealists.

Elena wanted to come with Arkady and Victor to Sparrow Hills.

"It's too dangerous, Elena. It's police business, and the Werewolves know who you are by now."

"I can decide for myself what's too dangerous and what's not. I've seen a lot more of the Werewolves than either you or Victor."

Arkady had expected hostility, or at the very least a low level hum of threat and entitlement, but in fact the atmosphere was jovial and relaxed. Men chatted, admired each other's bikes, and swigged beer from cans. Beer didn't really count as alcohol in a country where men drank vodka and real men drank brake fluid. A couple of the Werewolves recognized Arkady and Victor, but no one held their gaze too long or raised their voice too loud.

"Officers of the law, I presume?"

There it was, Arkady thought, just when he had thought it might not come at all.

The speaker was small and tanned, his skin the texture of leather and his hair twisted into a white rat's tail which hung between his shoulder blades. He was sitting on a low wall where several antique guns had been laid out. There were pistols, rifles, even flintlocks and muskets.

"Yours?" Arkady asked.

"I'm a collector." The man reached out a hand. "Dima Balakin."

"May I?"

"Please."

Arkady picked up the rifle and turned it over in his hands. A .33, as he'd known it would be. Alex was shot with a .33 rifle and motorcycle tire marks were found near his body. Coincidence? Or was it confidence to the point of insolence, the kind of thing done by a man who knows he will never be brought to trial. He had the distinct impression of being toyed with, the one man in the whole place unaware that he was the butt of a joke.

He could take the weapon as evidence, but that might risk an adverse reaction. A quick glance at Victor confirmed it.

"I just bought an old 1940s Mosin-Nagant," Victor said.

"Aha!" Dima's eyes lit up with the joy one connoisseur finds in another's company. "A man who knows what he's talking about."

"Some guns are works of art."

"It's true. I have a few that are that old, and even older than that," said Dima.

Victor and Elena started to browse through the guns. Arkady looked at Dima's bike, all black and crouching low to the ground as it leaned on its kickstand.

"Beautiful machine, no?" Dima said.

"Striking." It looked like something from a sci-fi movie. It was a little too retro for a cutting-edge cyclist to ride. The wheels were as blacked-out as the chassis, and large rigid panniers over the back axle gave it haunches and menace.

"Kortezh," Dima said. "Built for the presidential motorcade. There are a few left over, if you know where to find them."

Arkady crouched down by the rear tire, pretending to admire the beast from ground level. From behind the wheel, he brought out his phone and took a quick picture of the tire's tread.

"Get what you were looking for?" Dima asked as Arkady stood up. Dima went on before Arkady could answer. "While you're here, you should meet Yashin."

Yashin was the leader of the Werewolves.

"Of course."

"Come with me. He's much in demand, but I'm his right-hand man, so to speak."

Dima led the three of them through what felt like concentric circles of men and machines. The smell of sweat and engine oil was overwhelming. Arkady kept Elena between himself and Victor. He was aware that men were looking her up and down, but if Elena was scared, she didn't show it.

Yashin was in the middle of the innermost circle, sitting on his bike with his feet resting on the handlebars. Arkady had seen armchairs smaller than the seat. It went upwards and curled around all at once, so that when Yashin leaned back against it, he looked like a monarch on his throne. No Russian-made motorcycle could ever look this good, Arkady thought. He noticed a small circle on the trim just below the handlebars where the manufacturer's logo had been painted over, presumably to disguise the fact that this bike was in fact German.

Yashin raised an eyebrow when he saw Dima arrive with Arkady, Elena, and Victor. He uncoiled himself and dropped to the ground. His look was full-on, almost clichéd biker gang aesthetic: heavy black boots, thick black leather trousers, and a black sleeveless leather jacket with the club's flaming wolf's head emblem emblazoned across the front. The true north arrow of a knife scar ran up his right cheek, and he was missing his left arm.

"Ironic, huh?" Yashin said. "Named after the most famous goalkeeper of all when you've only got one arm." Arkady got the feeling this was a standard opening for him. He remembered Lev Yashin, dressed all in black and nicknamed the "Black Spider" for his reach and saves. For twenty years he had manned the goal for Dynamo Moscow and the Soviet Union, less a man than a magnetic field, attracting shots to himself. Yashin had made the position of goalkeeper uniquely dynamic and sexy.

"How did you lose it?" Arkady asked the obvious question.

"Industrial accident. Car crash. Infectious disease. Who cares? Watch." Dima tossed a can of beer fast and high, and in the blink of an eye he had taken three steps across and plucked it out of the air with what would have been the wrong, less natural hand if only he'd had two. "I was as good as the original, no question. Perhaps he should have been named after me."

He laughed loudly, inviting them to be part of the joke. His charisma was inclusive, Arkady thought, a bombast who let you think that he was in on the joke too. Lebedev's charisma was of a different kind, the eye patch aside; more brooding, less fun. And Yashin, surrounded by his men, seemed untouchable in a way Lebedev could never be.

Yashin turned to Elena. "I'm sorry about your friend and I swear that no one from my organization was responsible for his death. If you want, I'll help you in any way I can."

None of this was suspicious, Arkady thought. He and Victor had been here at the last Forum demonstration, Alex's death had been on the news, so it would have been surprising if Yashin *hadn't* known about it.

"Thank you," she said.

"But"—Yashin held his hand up, index finger pointing to the sky—"that doesn't change the fact that Forum is a misguided and dangerous organization. I understand your idealism but believe me when I tell you that if you had your way, the country as we know it would cease to exist. No one who loves this country can think the way you do."

Elena was not cowed. "I love this country just as much as you. That's why I want to see it change."

"You kids always think the moment you gain political consciousness is Year Zero." Arkady realized from the way Yashin was talking that he must be nearing sixty, but he looked age-

78

less. "The Soviet Union was the most powerful empire in the world. No, don't give me any crap about America. Did America extend across twelve time zones? Did America unite fifteen republics into one? Did America rescue the Baltics from the Nazis, give the Moldovans a place in the world, educate some barbaric Tajiks?

"Then," he continued, "without a single shot, it was over. We lost everything we had for bubble gum and jeans. And McDonald's. Your friends from the police here will remember Moscow after the fall: empty shops, seven-hour queues to buy basic groceries with coupons. All the old values were lost. I always hated these pretenders who became capitalists overnight. And homosexuality, which had always been a sin— which had always been a mental illness, *actually*—was legalized. Now they even allow gays to take marriage in church! Suddenly everyone loved us. All the other countries, when we were lying in the dirt, they loved us. And now, because of Vladimir Putin, after thirty long years we're back and strong again. Some of us, the true patriots, stand firm against global Satanism, the rush to consumerism that denies all spirituality, the destruction of traditional values, all this homosexual talk, this Western democracy. And guess what? No one likes us anymore. Good. Wonderful. You know your history, young lady? Have you heard of the ancient Roman emperor Caligula? '*Oderint dum metuant*,' he said. 'Let them hate, so long as they fear.'"

He reached down and flicked a piece of dirt off his boot. "Now, if you'll excuse me, it's time for the ride to start."

"I hope we haven't kept you," Victor said with sarcasm.

"Not at all. The ride starts when I say it starts."

He climbed back onto his bike and turned the key. The noise from the engine was deafening.

The crowd around Yashin parted as, one-handed, he eased out through the throng and onto the road. His bike was heavy, one that would require most riders to steer with two hands, but he made it look easy riding with just one. The Werewolves followed him.

A cat wandered out of the crowd and into the street.

"Here, kitty." Victor was single-minded when it came to cats. "Here, kitty, kitty."

"Victor, the cat's okay," Arkady said.

Bikes were coming thick and fast now. Victor ran into the street after the cat, but Dima was there first. He scooped up the cat, swayed back to avoid a claw in the face, and put it down gently on the far pavement.

"That was an old cat," Victor said. "Thank you. He would never have made it to the other side."

"I'm not sure you would have either," said Dima.

14

Arkady called up the case file on Alex's murder when he got back to Petrovka. Victor took Arkady's phone and performed some wizardry which ensured that within two minutes the photograph Arkady had taken of Dima's tire was coming out of the printer. Arkady found the picture that forensics had taken of the tire track in Gorky Park and laid the two next to each other.

It was the same tire tread. There was no doubt about it.

"What about the gun?" Arkady said.

"The rifle you were looking at?"

"Yes."

"Last time that was fired, Brezhnev and his eyebrows were in the Kremlin."

★　★　★

Dima had been in and out of Lefortovo Prison, so often it was as if the prison were Dynamo Stadium and he had a season ticket for all the games. Arkady counted thirty-two separate offenses in as many years, leading to fourteen separate stints inside. It was rare to see a man in any line of work who displayed such commitment to his craft. His details were in the system, along with his address.

He lived in a micro district. You could find this kind of housing on the outskirts of every post-Soviet city, usually near the airport and always near subway and bus stations to make it easy for people who lived there to get to work. They were packed with stalagmite tower blocks in shades of gray and white and were made from components prefabricated in factories before being slotted together like a city of Lego. There was no day too sunny, no mood too joyous, and no smile too wide that could not be extinguished by five minutes in one of these soulless vacuums. Arkady gave silent thanks that he didn't have to live in one of them. Not yet, at any rate.

"I was wondering when you would come," Dima said as he opened the door to them.

He led them inside. The place was spotless; cabinets on the walls full not just of antique guns but cap badges, medals, hip flasks, and more.

"My father was a veteran," Dima said, and it was all there in those five words; a love, a way of life, disappointment, and pride in equal measures across the generations.

Arkady showed him the photos. "They match."

"They do," Dima agreed.

"But I feel there's a 'but' coming."

"You feel correctly."

"Go on."

"I wasn't riding it."

"Can you prove that?"

"In a manner of speaking."

He took his phone out, scrolled back a little way through the camera roll, and handed it to Arkady. "Start from there. Look at the time stamps."

The first photo was of Dima in a bar with some friends, a group selfie, taken at 9:04 p.m. on the evening Alex had called Arkady. He swiped through. Drinking games, 10:37 p.m. One man passed out while another made a stupid expression, 11:23 p.m. Blurred streetlights, 1:01 a.m. The bedroom of what looked like a brothel, 2:46 a.m.: an overhead light without a shade, a young woman with bright red lipstick and a void behind her eyes; 2:49 a.m., a line of cocaine on a table; 3:12 a.m., a video of him having sex with the young woman, with her encouraging him as though he were a racehorse nearing the winning post. Arkady saw that the video lasted almost two minutes and moved on to the next pictures. Some more drinking, this time with a couple of new people who hadn't been there before: 4:16 a.m., 5:24 a.m., 6:02 a.m. Whenever Dima's face appeared in the photos, he looked so drunk that Arkady was impressed he could still stand. Then a café for breakfast, 7:11 a.m.

"Location services are on, so you can see where they all were taken," Dima said.

That was beyond Arkady's technical ability. He handed the phone to Victor, who showed him how it worked. Arkady conjured a map in his head, placing Dima at specific points in time and space across the night. At no time could Dima have gotten to Alex and killed him in Gorky Park, even if he had been sober.

"Then who took your bike?" Arkady said. Dima shrugged. "Because whoever it was, you had it back by today."

"Werewolves borrow each other's bikes all the time. We're very much a brotherhood, you know. We have a slogan, 'What's mine is ours.' Bikes, women, vodka. We're very communist."

"Do you know who had your bike that night?"

"As a matter of fact, I don't."

"Would you tell us if you did?"

"Of course not."

15

There were around a hundred people at the string quartet's concert, enough to make it seem like a good crowd and small enough to feel intimate. Arkady tried to make himself enjoy the concert and appreciate the quartet as an ensemble, but he had trouble looking away from Elena. She looked beautiful dressed in dark green and with her hair pulled back into one long braid. He sat near the back so he wouldn't distract her, though he knew she was too professional to let her attention wander.

The piece was dissident and melodic at the same time, but music was never just music. For him, it evoked memories of the past, places he had been and people who he had loved. He had to admit that Parkinson's played with his emotions and might have something to do with the way his eyes teared up as he listened.

———

He drove her home afterward.

"It's funny," she said. "I love being second violin. Being first violin suited Karina and being second suites me. All four of us are supposed to be equal, of course, but it never works that way. There's a reason they call it 'playing second fiddle.' It's always said as an insult, but it shouldn't be. It's the bridge between the leading first violin and the other instruments."

He lost his footing on the way up the stairs to her apartment. It was a sudden thing, unexpected. He looked down and his feet seemed miles away, as though he were looking through the wrong end of a telescope. He reached for where he thought the step must be, but how could he control such distant limbs? Then he was falling, arms out in front of him and Elena grabbed for him. With her help, he pushed himself upright and recovered his balance.

"Are you okay?" she asked.

"Yes."

"What happened?"

"I don't know. I slipped. Second time today."

He navigated the remaining stairs moving deliberately and slowly.

Once in the apartment, he collapsed onto the couch.

Elena made tea and poured out two cups for them.

"Now," she said, "what happened there?"

"What happened where?"

"On the stairs."

"I slipped."

"You looked like you fell, not slipped. And I saw the way you went up the rest of the stairs. You're not drunk, that much is clear."

"No, I'm not drunk. Just tired."

"Do you always fall over when you're tired?"

"Sometimes."

"Then you must be a mass of bruises. Tell me," she said.

"Tell you what?"

"Tell me what's wrong with you."

"Nothing's wrong with me."

She sipped her tea and regarded him over the rim of her tea cup. She neither smiled nor moved, did nothing to put him at his ease. Arkady was amused. It was one of the interrogator's oldest tricks, using silence as a weapon.

"I have Parkinson's disease," he said.

It was a stigma. He hadn't thought of it that way before, but of course it was. Why else, his own denial apart, would he not have told anybody else about it? The moment he told someone about his diagnosis, their perception of who he was would change. Everyone cares about the opinion of others, and Arkady was no different. He didn't want to be treated as though he were an invalid. He had always assumed he was healthier than the average Russian male—not, he had to concede, an especially high bar. She put her hand on his knee.

"I know a few people who have it. Elderly relatives back in Kyiv. I learned certain coping strategies that they could use."

"Did they listen to you?"

"Less than they should. More than they might."

"What are the strategies?"

"Exercising."

Arkady rolled his eyes. "I was married to a gymnast once. She told me I needed to exercise more. I had always enjoyed different forms of exercise, but once it became her project, I lost all interest."

"You don't like being told what to do."

"You're right. What else should I be doing?"

"Getting enough sleep and rest."

"I know that's true."

"Turning to prayer."

He let that pass.

"Talking about it."

"A problem shared is a problem halved?"

"Exactly."

"Well, I'm talking about it to you now, aren't I?"

"I bet I'm the first, right?"

"You are."

"You could tell Zhenya. You could tell Victor."

"I could but I haven't. If I tell them, they'll hover over me like mother hens."

"You don't think anybody has caught on? You don't think that people who care about you don't wonder?"

"Maybe. Anything else?"

"As in coping strategies?"

"Yes."

"Most important of all, I think, is maintaining a sense of humor."

"That I can agree with."

———

It was Arkady's quest to find Karina which had first brought him to this apartment, and Karina's continued absence was the reason—part of the reason, anyway—that he was here now. Circumstances had subtly changed. For the time being, Elena lived alone, just as Arkady did. Karina might walk through the door any minute. It was conceivable that Tatiana could walk through his door, but he doubted it would happen. Being alone was not the same as being lonely. Being alone often meant not having to suffer fools. There were few freedoms more precious than that. He missed Tatiana but he hoped that soon he would adjust to the empty apartment

As if reading his mind, Elena said, "I love Karina's company. But sometimes, even before she disappeared, when I'd come back here, turn the key in the lock, and see the lights were off and there was nobody home, I was relieved. It's not that I didn't want her there; I didn't want *anyone* there. I could do what I wanted."

"Would you rather I was gone?" Arkady asked.

"No, don't go. Stay the night."

Surprised, he paused, then reached across and pulled her close. He kissed the soft contours of her face, then her mouth. How it happened, he wasn't sure. They lowered themselves to the cool hardwood floor.

"Do you know how beautiful you are?" he whispered. He slipped off her dress, then his own clothes. She stretched as he slowly caressed each breast with his mouth.

Finally, he covered her body with his. Her skin was smooth as warm sandstone. They rocked in each other's arms until he could stand it no more and he entered her, grasping her buttocks with one hand, the back of her head with the other.

He lay on his back afterward. Elena's head was on his chest, her leg thrown across his. He reached up to the couch, pulled down pillows and a blanket, and covered the two of them.

Just a short time ago, he had wondered if life was worth living. How was it that the simple act of making love could make such a difference? He drifted off to sleep.

Arkady's cell phone rang in the dark. He woke, fumbled for the phone, dropped it, scrabbled on the floor, and just when his fingers closed around it, it stopped ringing. He looked at the screen. **Zhenya**, it said. There were several reasons Zhenya could be calling in the middle of the night, and none of them were good.

The phone rang again.

"Zhenya?" Arkady asked.

"Lebedev's been assassinated."

16

The order came down from on high that the investigation into Lebedev's murder was to be given highest priority. A joint task force comprising all relevant agencies was established, and together the finest law enforcement personnel in the entire federation would work tirelessly, brilliantly, and in an exemplary multidisciplinary fashion to bring the perpetrators of this vile calumny to justice.

In other words, Arkady thought, it would be a muddle of competing agencies treading on each other's toes, fighting for turf, trying to claim all the credit and avoid any of the blame, and generally ensuring that any useful leads were lost either by accident or design in all the confusion—which was, of course, the whole point.

"Renko, you're going to represent the police on this task force." Zurin looked as though he were bestowing a great honor on him, possibly even the Order of Lenin, and looked a little put out that Arkady didn't seem grateful for the honor. "It makes sense, since you're already involved in the Alex Levin case and the Forum connection there. How's that going, by the way?"

It said everything about Zurin's attitude to Alex's murder that he should inquire so casually. If this had been a case in which he'd wanted to find the killer, he would have been all over Arkady several times a day, demanding updates, reports, lines of inquiry, and suspects.

"We found the motorcycle used in the attack. Unfortunately, the owner has a cast-iron alibi for that night," Arkady said.

"That is unfortunate."

"We're still looking for someone who might have used the motorcycle"

"Good, good. Keep on with that."

"It won't be easy if I have to spend all my time on the Lebedev case."

"No. I don't suppose it will be."

In the corner, Victor looked as if he was trying very hard not to laugh.

The task force incident room had been set up in the Kremlin itself. It was an appropriate location because Lebedev had been killed on the sidewalk in front of the Hotel National, and if Arkady crossed the room and looked out of the window, he could see the actual site covered over with forensic tents and sealed off with police cars at both ends.

There were two dozen people in the room that Arkady knew from previous investigations. He would stay silent, listen, and see what he could piece together in the margins. No one would tell him anything of use, at least not deliberately, but they might let something slip without realizing. In the same way that music was often played between the notes, truth could be found between the lines. Sometimes that was the only place it resided.

These were the facts that so far had been established: Leonid Lebedev had been walking toward the Hotel National just after midnight. He had been alone, even though a Forum member had been murdered only a few days before. Lebedev shunned security when he could and tended to use it only at rallies and public meetings. He liked to be accessible, to move around the city just like an ordinary citizen rather than a politician removed from the masses.

The FSB must have been watching him for months. They knew where he lived and how he lived. Lebedev being anyplace at any time would not have been a surprise to them because they were always with him. They might as well have introduced themselves.

Lebedev had been walking on the left side against the flow of traffic rather than with it. A man on a motorcycle rode toward him, from Red Square heading south. He slowed and fired four shots at Lebedev from no more than six or seven feet: two to the head, one to the torso near the heart, and a fourth that grazed his right arm. The accuracy of the first three shots suggested that this last one caused only a superficial wound because Lebedev was already falling. The bullets came from a standard Makarov pistol.

Arkady understood that some of this information was guesswork. A municipal street-cleaning truck had been parked on the street, and at the moment of the attack both Lebedev and the motorcyclist were obscured from the security camera's view. Only one camera was operational. In normal circumstances, there would have been several cameras on both sides of the street, but supposedly these had been turned off for routine maintenance. The only camera that had been turned on belonged to a TV company in a building two hundred feet away, a distance which would have made the footage unclear even without the street-cleaning truck. The motorcyclist turned around after the attack and retraced his route to the north.

The street, like every other street within three thousand feet of the Kremlin, was under constant surveillance. The idea that all the security cameras would be turned off at the same time and that a street-cleaning vehicle would be allowed to stop there was suspicious, to say the least. And why would the motorcyclist do a U-turn after the attack unless he knew that to continue south was to risk coming close enough to a security camera to be recognizable? The quickest, most obvious thing to do was to get out of there as fast as possible, which meant continuing in the direction he was heading.

Four tourists had been coming out of the hotel, a married couple and two men who didn't know each other or the couple. They had all been interviewed and their statements taken. None of them saw anything that could identify the motorcyclist; no number plate, no description of the bike beyond the most generic. The driver of the street cleaner had pulled over for a short nap, having been on shift for almost eighteen hours at the time, and was awakened by the gunshots. They all attempted to help Lebedev as he lay on the ground, but he was dead before they reached him.

If Arkady was right, the FSB were there to check that the operation went smoothly. If Lebedev had survived the initial attack, one of them would have finished him off while "helping."

Five Chechen nationals at three separate addresses were arrested early in the morning on suspicion of involvement. One was killed while resisting arrest. The other four were being questioned in custody and their statements would be made available eventually. This was standard procedure.

None of them had anything to do with the murder, Arkady was sure. They all were wanted for various other crimes that they may or may not have committed, but there was so little evidence that even the FSB couldn't have them arrested. This was the next best thing. Lock up Chechens for crimes they hadn't committed, safe in the knowledge that they probably hadn't been locked up for things they had done. And the man "shot resisting arrest" would have been a straight case of execution.

The briefing ended.

The leader of the task force asked, "Are there any questions?"

Somewhat to his surprise, Arkady found himself raising his hand.

"Investigator Renko, prosecutor's office. I would like to interview the suspects and the witnesses myself."

Even as he spoke, he wondered why he was doing this. Probably because most of the proceedings were such a farce. He didn't expect an answer in the affirmative, and he didn't get one.

"That won't be necessary."

"It may not be necessary, but is it possible?"

"No, it won't be possible either."

Arkady waited on the bank while Yashin swam. Borisovskiye Prudy Park hummed with activity behind him. There were football pitches, playgrounds, tennis courts, skateboard parks—but Arkady remembered when this had just been a pond where trees were mirrored in the water and where fishermen sat from dawn to dusk to avoid their wives.

How could a man swim with only one arm? Rather well, as it turned out. Yashin's arm emerged and disappeared in hypnotic rhythm, and from the wake left by his legs Arkady could see that he was constantly correcting course to compensate for being pulled to one side.

Yashin turned and headed for shore. Arkady had been waiting for an hour. He could happily wait another hour. The sun was on his face and for a while he could forget the investigation. There was nothing for him to do at Petrovka. All things considered, he'd rather be here.

Yashin stood up in the shallows. Water trailed off him as he walked the last few steps. He seemed taller than he had at Sparrow Hills, and the muscles of his chest were plates. Tattoos chased each other over his skin: dragons, stars, the gold onion domes of St. Basil's. And wolves, of course, peering around the side of his ribs and leaping across his shoulder blades.

"Have you been waiting long?"

Arkady stood up to greet him.

Yashin adjusted the silver crucifix around his neck. "I swim here every day. This place is one of my favorites. The peasants built dams here to breed fish that they could sell to the tsar's kitchens. Did you know that?"

"I didn't."

"And they were still breeding carp here until Brezhnev's time."

"Amazing."

"Forgive me. You haven't come to discuss pisciculture with me, I'm sure."

"I'm working on two murder cases now."

"Lebedev being the second one?"

"Yes."

"My offer of help stands."

"Your man Dima's motorcycle was used in the Alex Levin case. Lebedev was also killed by a man on a motorcycle with similar tire tracks.

"Dima has told you that he wasn't riding that night."

"He has."

"And forgive me again, the motorcycle in front of the Hotel National was one of ours too?"

"I don't know yet. The tracks were similar but not definitive."

"Then I'm not sure how I can help you."

"You could give me a list of your members."

"If you come with a warrant, I'd be delighted to."

Could Arkady get a warrant? It would depend on who the judge was. But even if he did get one, and even if Yashin did hand over the list, how much good would it do? He and Victor could interview the members one by one, but that would take forever. And these men were always on the move, they would cover for each other, they were protected. A list of members would look good in a report, but it would represent little more than a series of wild-goose chases.

"Who can join the Werewolves?"

"Anyone. Do you ride? I'd be delighted to consider your application."

"I don't, no. Not regularly, at any rate. Anyone?"

"Anyone. Well, apart from women. It's a men's club. No junkies. And no homosexuals either."

"Why can't gay men join?"

Yashin looked incredulous. "I don't even know what to say. Gays are not normal. You're not one yourself, are you, Investigator?"

"No, but I don't care if someone else is."

"Then you are a man of no faith."

"That's true, perhaps."

"We are Orthodox people. If one loses his faith in the Wolves or in Orthodoxy, life is meaningless. God is with us and God helps us. When we fought in Crimea, I saw miracles, many miracles. I saw bombed churches where people survived. I myself left a place thirty seconds before it was destroyed by a Ukrainian missile. Pulverized it. They would have had to scrape my body parts out of the trees. But my faith protected me. This is a religious and spiritual war we're fighting, Investigator, and the soul of Russia is at stake."

Yes, Arkady thought, a war was exactly what it was, but a war against foes perceived as well as real, internal opponents as well as external enemies. It was Stalin's Great Terror updated for modern times, with disinformation, legal machinations, indiscriminate violence. Bloodshed was a way of proving loyalty. One was either with or against. And the penalties for resistance were changing all the time, from imprisonment to death, ordered or merely allowed to happen. It amounted to the same thing.

17

Hundreds followed Lebedev's funeral route all the way to Vagankovskoye Cemetery, most of them wearing green face paint
or green clothing as requested. Putin had evidently decided
that the procession should take place peacefully, not so much
out of decency as his desire not to make Lebedev a martyr. Besides, they could hardly announce a special task force into his
murder and then deny him a proper funeral.

Vagankovskoye had first been established for the burial of
plague victims in the eighteenth century. It had been placed
outside the city walls at the time to stop the spread of disease.
Arkady looked around the mourners. The FSB were there, of
course. Funerals were the one place they could really blend in
with their dark suits and dark glasses. Arkady watched them
watching Elena.

A winding walkway stretched in front of him. Tombstones
were decorated with carvings of golden eagles, maple leaves,

and boxing gloves. Pine needles were woven into wreaths. Photographs of generals and divas stared out from frames on granite. There were sculptures of Soviet heroes and cosmonauts, a white marble ballet dancer balanced *en pointe*, and a popular comedian sat with his dog. Death was everywhere. He shivered suddenly in the warm sun and remembered how Tatiana had always laughed and said "Shadow on your grave" when that happened.

Once the crowd had settled in their seats, someone in formal attire and a green eye patch strode to the microphone.

"We mourn the death of Leonid Lebedev, a man of honor who sought justice in the world. He was not just a leader for those of us who want to see change; he was a beloved friend."

Elena wiped tears away with the back of her hand.

More speeches followed, some emotional, some humorous, and all of them in one way or another praised Lebedev's work at Forum.

Arkady stayed at the wake with Elena as long as she could stand to be there, and then he took her home. His apartment this time, not hers.

"I don't know how safe you'll be at your place. I'd like you to stay with me, at least for the time being."

"Are you sure?"

"Of course. We can go and get some of your stuff tomorrow."

"What I don't understand is why wasn't Karina there today. She must have heard about Leonid's murder. Maybe she's dead too."

"It's odd, but I'll find out where she is. I don't think she's dead."

"Thank you for coming with me today. Did you think you might catch sight of the killer?"

"I wanted to see who was there."

"And did you?"

"Only the FSB. Of course, anyone could have been hiding behind the green face paint."

Once in the apartment, Elena walked straight to the bedroom and lay on the bed. Arkady lay down beside her and shifted her head to his shoulder. Exhausted, she closed her eyes and slept.

★　★　★

The next morning Arkady made coffee and toast for Elena. "There's something I should tell you," she said.

"What's that?"

"Does the name Uzeir Osmanov mean anything to you?"

"I've heard it before, but I can't place it."

"He's head of the Crimean Tatars. He lives in exile in Kyiv."

"That's it. And you must know him."

"Yes. He's my father."

"Oh. Why didn't you tell me before?"

"It's kept secret. He's a controversial figure here, so, for safety's sake, I haven't told anyone. Now that Leonid's dead, I think you should know. He was a good friend to Leonid. That's why I joined Forum in the first place."

"Did your father work with Leonid?"

"Yes. They had a cooperation pact, which they didn't publicize for obvious reasons. Of course, both were against the regime, they split donations when necessary to make sure that both movements had enough to work with, and they discussed strategies together."

"I assume your father knows what's happened."

"He knew right away. I spoke with him earlier today. He's desperate to find Leonid's killer and he wonders if you can help him go through all his records of their discussions and correspondence, just in case there's something there. If it's too much trouble, then just say no, but you're an investigator and you might see something that he's missed. He can't come here, obviously. He would be arrested the moment he set foot on Russian soil. We would have to go there."

Arkady thought about his investigation into Alex's death. Alex had been one of Leonid's followers and the two deaths could be related. Would Zurin allow him to travel as part of his investigation? Of course. Zurin disliked him so much, he would send him back to Siberia if he could. And what about Bronson's daughter? He guessed that maybe, because she was Elena's friend, there might be a connection there too. Or was he just rationalizing because he wanted to go?

"I'm not sure it's safe to go right now," Arkady said.

"I heard the Russians are starting to withdraw troops from the borders," said Elena.

"Why would they do that?"

"Some say they're giving in to foreign pressure; others say they're regrouping after heavy losses. But besides all that, my father is getting old. I want to see him while I can."

"Okay. Let me think about it."

It wasn't as simple as just flying direct to Kyiv. There were no flights anymore—not when it looked like Russia was withdrawing simply to marshal troops for an invasion. They'd have to go via a third country, and the most popular routes were via Minsk or Warsaw.

"I've always wanted to go back to Warsaw," he said.

"You have?"

"My mother was born in Warsaw and I remember happy times there with my grandparents. So let me look into flights."

"That's not going to be possible."

"Why not?"

"I can't fly."

"Can't, or won't?"

"They're the same thing in my case. Offer me a million rubles and I still couldn't get on a plane."

"So how are we going to get there?"

"Drive?"

18

Arkady called Victor before he left.

"You're *what*?"

"Elena and I will be driving to Kyiv to see her father," he repeated.

"You've really fallen for her, haven't you? I always knew you were crazy, but this takes the cake. Why not wait till the fighting actually starts? It might be even more fun."

"Apparently, the Russians have pulled back from the border. I don't think we'll have trouble."

"Are you stupid? They left plenty of troops there. They just stepped out for a tea break. They'll be back with more troops. How do you think they'll react when they see you have a Tatar woman with you—because there's no mistaking that—and what do you think they'll do to her when they find out she's the daughter of Uzeir Osmanov?"

"They won't."

"I can't believe you're doing this. Did you tell Zurin?"

"Of course. He couldn't be happier to see me go."

"And Zhenya?"

"He wanted to come with us and join Zelensky's army."

"Figures. I'll look in on him."

"Thanks, Victor."

★　★　★

They argued even before setting off.

"Are you sure you can drive?" Elena asked.

"Yes, of course."

"It's just that . . ."

"This is one of the reasons I don't tell people. Sooner or later they treat you like an invalid."

"Arkady, you fell on my stairs."

"So?"

"So driving a car is a whole lot more dangerous than climbing stairs."

"You're worried about road safety? In Russia?"

She lifted her hands and conceded the point.

"It comes and goes, you know, but I don't have trouble driving."

"You mean the symptoms come and go?"

"Yes. I can go for days at a time feeling fine, then something will come on me out of the blue. Then it goes away again."

"Like a change in the weather."

"Not exactly."

Elena flicked around the radio stations. Reception wasn't good, but she finally found a rap station and settled on that. He tolerated it for a few minutes, then reached over and turned it off.

"I'm sorry, I can't stand rap."

Annoyed, she said nothing for the next few miles.

He decided to change the mood.

"Tell me something. Do you think I'm too old for you?"

"Too old?"

"Well, I am a hundred and ten years old."

She laughed. "No, I like that you're older. You're grown up, unlike other men I've gone out with. You don't have to prove yourself. You just are. Maybe I should be asking you. Am I too young for you?"

"No such thing."

She laughed again.

"Now, I know you don't like rap, but you have to like this."

She opened her purse and brought out a CD.

"I hope this car is old enough to have a CD player."

"It is."

"This won the Eurovision Song Contest," she said. "No, don't look like that. It's called '1944,' and the chorus comes from an old folk song which every Crimean Tatar knows."

Arkady recognized the sound of the duduk, a wooden flute, at the start. The melody and the drone played beneath it, insistent and haunting. The musicians were channeling the pain of their ancestors. The singer sang in urgent staccato, switching from English to Tatar and back again, spinning out her tale, and when she neared the end, her voice broke.

"You can't teach that," Elena said. "The way she ends the song. Did you like it?"

He chose his words carefully: "I think it's extraordinary."

"I'm glad." She pressed a button on the CD player, and the song began again.

The highway unrolled beneath their wheels. Traffic was light and they made good time.

"I'm sorry you didn't get to go back to Warsaw. Why do you remember it as a happy time?"

"My grandparents were delighted to spend time with me and my mother. They seldom had the opportunity."

"They never visited you in Moscow?"

"No. They didn't get along with my father."

"Why?"

"He was cruel to my mother, and they could see that."

"What was your mother like?"

"She was brave. She wouldn't back down and he punished her for that. The crazy thing was that he was in love with her. She was beautiful and men were drawn to her. Of course, that drove him out of his mind."

The general wasn't above hitting his mother, and Arkady had always felt guilty for not being able to protect her. Maybe that was why Tatiana had left. She had constantly put herself in dangerous situations for the newspaper and he had constantly tried to stop her. She felt smothered by him and she left.

★   ★   ★

They passed signs for Selyatino, and Naro-Fominsk, towns unknown to Arkady. After a few hours they reached Obninsk, where they swapped places and Elena drove.

Arkady studied the directions Victor had sent him.

"In about three hours we're going to reach Bryansk. I'll take over then. I think we have to change to A240 to avoid a road closure." Victor had said that the road was closed by Russian soldiers. Not a good sign.

He sat back and gazed at rivers that wound in and around green farmland.

Time could go in two directions at once. Heading toward the future was also heading toward the past. During the Second World War, Arkady's father had fought both the Nazis and the Ukrainians, who at that time were seeking their independence from what was the Soviet Union. Long months of summer turned to autumn, then winter, as campaigns were conducted with no regard for human life. The Butcher of Ukraine, they called him, and General Renko had worn the moniker with pride.

"That's what you need in life," he had told Arkady. "The will to do what others won't, the fortitude to rinse yourself in blood rather than wash it off."

The General had never had any time for Americans, except for one. "Patton," he said. "Now, there's a man who understood war. He would say, 'No bastard ever won a war by dying for his country.'"

Every man walks in his father's footsteps one way or another, and these were so bloody, they squelched.

"Arkady?"

He snapped back to the present. "Sorry, are we stopping?"

"We need gas."

"Okay, you wait here."

Glad for a little activity, he walked inside the station, picked up some chips and sodas, paid 4,500 rubles for the gas and snacks, and came back out to find Elena stretching with one hand on the top of the car and the other lifting her ankle back behind her knee.

He started pumping gas. "Are you a runner?" he asked.

"No, just stiff. How much longer do you think?"

"About eight hours, I'd say."

She groaned.

"I'll drive. We're close to Bryansk, only ninety-five miles from the Ukranian border."

"I'll visit the restroom first."

Back in the car, Elena fell asleep almost immediately. Some people could fall asleep anywhere, anytime they wanted. It was an art.

Arkady followed Victor's directions and drove four more hours on the M3, then took E101 to Konotop. According to classic literature, every second woman in Konotop was a witch. That fact alone roused his curiosity, and he decided they should stay the night.

Elena was now awake.

"Let's sleep in an actual bed tonight," he said.

He found a cheery-looking hotel that was still decorated with Christmas lights.

Their room was plain but had the added luxury of a bathroom with a shower. Elena flopped onto the bed, too tired to take her clothes off. Arkady dropped down beside her and undressed her but he couldn't resist kissing her as he did so.

"I'm tired, really tired. Aren't you?" she said.

"I'm waking up." He continued kissing her down the length

of her body, then, finally taking sympathy, he lifted her up and tucked her in under the covers.

In the middle of the night, he sat up in bed. An old woman with a smile rocked backed and forth in her chair. He stared while she stared back and continued rocking and smiling but saying nothing. Was this one of the witches come to visit? He threw his pillow at her. Nothing there. Feeling like a fool, he retrieved his pillow and fell back to bed.

After a breakfast of coffee and corn porridge, they set out for Kyiv.

"I had a hallucination last night. An old woman sitting in the corner of our room. She was a benign witch."

"How could you tell?"

"She was smiling. So interesting, the mind. It's as if there's another dimension to this life that we aren't aware of when we're awake but it's there all the time. It breaks out in dreams or, in my case, hallucinations."

"Kind of creepy."

KYIV

19

The drive was short, and as they crossed the bridge into the city, Arkady was struck by the view to his right. Steep bluffs covered with pine trees rose hundreds of feet above the banks of the Dnieper River, and at the top, golden domes, church spires, and apartment buildings peaked through the trees.

They drove to the center of the city on a winding road that finally led to Kyiv's main avenue, Khreshchatyk Street. It was lined with red brick and pretty pastel-colored buildings. He turned onto Stanislavs'koho Street and parked in front of number 3, Uzeir's apartment building.

Elena and Arkady had to show their passports to the doorman in the lobby and again to the man standing outside the apartment door on the top floor.

"Good to see you again, Marko," Elena said. "This is Investigator Renko from Moscow."

Marko Kravets was almost a foot shorter than Arkady,

twenty years younger, and considerably balder, and he wore glasses, but the grip in his handshake conveyed great strength. Arkady had come across plenty of bodyguards in his time and he knew that it was the small ones who were often the most effective. Man mountains, who could stand in the aisle of a bus and touch both sets of windows at the same time, looked good on TV, but those who lacked the size had to make up for it with anticipation and discipline. Arkady had no doubt that Kravets could bend and twist someone twice his size as easily as he could breathe.

Kravets opened the door and ushered them in. Passages from the Koran had been framed and hung on the wall beside the Crimean Tatar flag. Uzeir was sitting at a small table, reading a newspaper. He looked up and caught sight of Elena. His face lit up. He pushed himself to his feet and drew his daughter to his chest. Arkady felt like a privileged bystander and unwelcome interloper at the same time.

"Papa," Elena said as she disentangled herself, "this is Arkady."

Uzeir's face was all creases and crevasses, lines scored with steppe dust and lagoon salt. A bump on his forehead marked where, over the years, he had bowed his head to the floor in prayer. He offered his hand.

"Thank you for coming," he said.

★　★　★

They spent the afternoon in Uzeir's study going through his correspondence with Leonid Lebedev. He had printed out all the emails and placed them in a ring binder. He brought out boxes filled with bank transfers, policy documents, and personal letters between himself and Leonid.

"Elena has vouched for you," he laughed. "Otherwise, I would no more share these with a Russian investigator than fly to the moon."

Arkady didn't tell him that the FSB had probably read them all anyway, and if they hadn't, they could do so anytime they wanted.

Elena and Uzeir retreated to a couch at the other end of the room where they could talk without disturbing Arkady. He went through all the paperwork and noticed that Karina Abakova's name appeared here and there on several of the business documents, but there really was nothing there, not that Arkady could see. He asked Uzeir for certain clarifications. Who was this person? Which meeting did this note refer to? But even those failed to provide evidence worth pursuing. Arkady reminded himself that this was the way it went on almost all investigations; endless trawling through information for no return. Clues didn't handily present themselves as such. They had to be sifted, refined, eked out, nuggets of gold in the silt, and there was always more silt than gold. He was disappointed.

"Have you found anything useful?" Elena asked.

"Nothing," he said. Uzeir's expression was crestfallen, and Arkady attempted to reassure him. "At least now I have a better understanding of what you and Leonid set out to accomplish when you created Forum. I'm not giving up."

Before leaving the study, Uzeir wanted to show Arkady the things he still kept, memories that he still held tight. He brought out a roll of cloth, unwrapping it slowly and carefully as a museum curator would when showing his artifacts to an honored guest. Out of one fold came a long *marama*, a head-scarf made of white silk embroidered with repeated patterns of the tree of life. Another unrolling revealed silver earrings, then a silk glove, then a bracelet and ring.

"Your wife's?" Arkady asked.

"Yes. Elena's mother. She died before we were allowed back." Uzeir dabbed at his eyes. "You must think me very sentimental," he said.

"Not at all," Arkady replied. "You said she died before you were allowed back. Back from where?"

"Uzbekistan. Let's have some tea. It's a long story and my mouth is dry. Elena, you've heard this story a hundred times, but I hope you will join us."

Uzeir poked his head into the kitchen to ask for the tea, then led Arkady and Elena to the living room.

A few minutes later a woman in a brightly embroidered dress entered the room carrying tea and biscuits on a round brass tray. As she poured the tea, the silver and gold baubles on her wrists jangled.

"Arkady, this is the lady who takes good care of me. Sarah is her name. And, Sarah, this is Arkady Renko, a good friend of Elena's."

Arkady rose to greet her. Elena gave her a long hug.

"Wonderful to see you," Sarah said.

"It's been a long time," said Elena. "Too long."

Once Sarah had left the room, Elena prompted her father to begin.

"How old were you when you left Crimea?"

Uzeir took a sip of his tea and smoothed the table's wooden surface as if it were sand.

"Generations of my family had lived and died in Crimea, but Russia wanted to be rid of us and move Russians in to become more than a minority of the country's population. I was seven years old when they came, old enough to remember it all—too young perhaps to appreciate the full horror, for which Allah be praised. Men in uniforms, or should I say, men in different uniforms? We'd had the Nazis, of course, but now they were gone, and in their place came Russians. 'NKVD,' people whispered. 'NKVD.' I didn't know that the 'NKVD' meant Russian secret police, but I knew they were bad and that they didn't like us.

"They accused us of having collaborated with the Nazis. That was another word I had to learn. We hadn't collaborated, of course, unless by 'collaboration' they meant going about our lives. The irony of it was that we behaved no differently with the Nazis than we did with the Soviets. We didn't want either of them there.

"It only took three days. Started on the eighteenth of May 1944, done by the twentieth. There were almost two hundred thousand Tatars in Crimea, and they deported every last one. Every man, woman, and child. They came with guns. 'Pack up your stuff, get on the trains, go.' The trains were meant for cattle, not humans. There were supposed to be fifty people in each car, maximum, but they crammed in a hundred, maybe a hundred and twenty, and there was no way we could escape because all the doors and windows were bolted shut. If you had food and water with you, then you guarded it with your life— literally. Disease—well, you could hardly have designed a better breeding ground for it, could you? At every stop they opened the doors and tossed the corpses out. That smell has never really left me. The rotting stench of death . . ." Uzeir sighed.

"Anyway, we ended up in Uzbekistan. The steppes are beautiful, you know. There's something in the endless sweep of the high plains that I love. But we had never asked to be taken there. And the locals were hardly thrilled to see us. They'd been told that we were traitors who had worked hand in glove with the fascists, and they didn't want us there any more than we wanted to be there. The moment I got off the train, a stone flew past my head and smashed against the side of the carriage. It was an Uzbek man, and he'd aimed directly at me. Who throws stones at a seven-year-old child?"

"No one," Arkady said.

"We called it the Sürgünlik, the Exile, and to this day there is no word in our language that evokes so much meaning: pride, suffering, endurance, and a terrible longing for home."

"How did you get back?" Arkady asked.

"In the fifties, Khrushchev gave Crimea to Ukraine and we were welcomed back. Then, after the Soviet Union was dissolved in 1991, we separated from Ukraine and became an independent country. Of course, Putin never forgot. He invaded Crimea in 2014. For the world, it was nothing. For Crimea, it was bad. For Crimea's Tatars, it was cataclysmic. Ten thousand of us fled, this time to Ukraine."

"And here we are again," said Elena, "June 2021, and Russia is trying to stamp us out again. I wonder where we can go if Russia invades Ukraine and wins."

"You should leave this whole part of the world, my darling,

because you're young, and with your music you will always be able to take care of yourself," Uzeir said. "But I'm going nowhere. I refuse to be bullied again."

★　　★　　★

The next morning Kyiv dazzled in the sunshine. Arkady and Elena had a day free while Uzeir was in meetings, and then he would be needing a nap. They decided to tour the city.

As they began walking, she said, "They say you can walk from one end of Kyiv to the other in the summertime without leaving the shade of a tree."

"I have to wonder why anyone would choose to live in Moscow instead of here."

"I wanted to stay, but I also wanted to play to larger audiences. Bigger city, more venues for music."

"Like the subway?"

Elena refused to take the bait. "Yes, like playing in the subway."

They walked until they reached the muddy shores of the Dnieper River.

"It's so wide."

"Wide and long. This is the river that divides Ukraine, north to south. It flows into the Baltic Sea in the south. If the Russians get their way, they'll annex the eastern side of the river just as they annexed Crimea."

"The river itself must be valuable to them."

"Absolutely. There are four or five hydroelectric power stations on it. That's all it can be used for now. You can't drink from it, you can't swim in it, you can't even wash your hands in it. It's polluted and still radioactive."

"From Chernobyl?"

"Yes. It's only ten miles away."

They turned back the way they had come. Arkady noticed sunlight bursting upon a tall steel statue in the distance.

"That's the *Mother Motherland* statue," Elena said.

They walked up a hill to the National Museum grounds. The statue wasn't hard to find. *Mother Motherland* stood tall and straight, holding her sword and shield aloft.

"People call her Brezhnev's daughter," Elena said.

Arkady walked up and read the plaque: "'In Honor of the Soviet Union's Victory in World War Two.' Impressive," he said.

They continued to walk until they reached Independence Square, just a few short blocks from Uzeir's apartment.

"I remember when it was just called Maidan," Arkady said.

"People sometimes still call it that, but after the Soviet Union fell and Ukraine declared itself independent from Russia, it became Independence Square."

The square spread out as an ellipse. At the center, a tall column of marble rested on a pedestal designed to look like a baroque Christian temple. A statue of Berehynia, the goddess and protector of Ukraine, stood at the very top holding a golden rose branch.

Elena led Arkady to the other side of the monument. There, a fountain rose up and around four powerful bronze statues.

"According to myth, those three warriors were the city's founders," Elena said. "Kyi, Shchek, and Khoryv."

Kyi was at the center, a large shield in his left hand. On either side of him, his two brothers stood, one lifting his bow, the other with his hand on a plow. Their sister, Lybid, rose above them with her arms spread wide.

"Kyiv is named after Kyi, the oldest brother."

"The girl isn't considered a founder?"

"I guess not. Newlyweds come to this place," Elena said. "If they throw flowers into the fountain, that's a sign they will have a long and happy marriage."

"Does it work?"

She gave him a look.

At the other end of the ellipse, a bronze statue of the archangel Michael stood with his gold-tipped wings above a replica of the city's medieval gates.

History had marched through these gates: Varangians, Mongols, and Tatars had come and gone, conquerors and in their own turn conquered.

"Were you here during the EuroMaidan Revolution?" Arkady asked.

"Yes, but Uzeir wouldn't let me out of our apartment. I snuck out a few times but couldn't get past the Ukrainian police. I heard all about it, though, and our apartment is so close that we could hear the protesters' chants and all the explosions that followed. You see that large white building with the pillars over there? That's the Conservatory, where the protesters gathered, ate, and slept."

"Also, a great vantage point to shoot from," Arkady said.

As Arkady remembered, it had all started because President Viktor Yanukovych led the people of Ukraine to believe they would be allowed to join the European Union. Putin called him to Moscow. He worried that Ukraine was leaning too far to the West and he nixed the idea.

The people of Ukraine were outraged. Protesters covered the square day and night. They started with signs and speeches, but when the police tried to evacuate them, they resisted by throwing rocks and Molotov cocktails. The protest escalated into violent clashes and fires, and by February 2014, five days after it started, more than a hundred people had died. Finally, Yanukovych fled the country and a new president was installed.

"It was called the 'Revolution of Dignity.' Soon after, Russia went to war with Crimea and annexed it." As if reminded, Elena looked at her watch. "Uzeir will be waiting for us. We better get back."

As they left the square, Berehynia and Michael watched over them, a goddess and an archangel standing guard over those who walked through its ancient gates.

Arkady hoped they were up to the job.

★　★　★

Uzeir had booked a table for seven o'clock at his favorite restaurant, a couple of blocks away. Kravets walked with them. He was assigned to Uzeir's protection by the SBU, the Security Service of Ukraine. Arkady saw that his eyes were never still; he was always watching, seeking, and assessing. Every approaching pedestrian was a threat and every passing vehicle was a menace until otherwise proven.

The city hummed. At outdoor tables, waitresses scurried between the pavement and the kitchen with trays of cocktails and bruschetta. Guests at a gallery's opening night clinked glasses and kissed air. BLACKWORK DONE HERE, said a tattoo parlor's sign below a picture of what looked like tribal markings from the Pacific Islands.

"Bulgakov used to live here, you know," Uzeir said.

"I didn't know. He wrote one of my favorite books, *The Master and Margarita*."

"Mine too."

Painted ravens soared across one entire exterior wall the size of a tennis court, a sole white one amid all the black like a glimmer of sunlight.

"There were real ravens here at one time. They belonged to Grisha, a mafia captain who ran a small crew of foot soldiers and reported to the godfather. He looked like a professor of literature, tall and tweedy, with glasses, and he used to come out with things that made me wonder how he'd ever been in the mafia, let alone done time. 'Love will always win,' that kind of thing. He had four ravens, and after he died some vandals broke into the cage and released the birds, but three of them, Korbin, Kirill, and Karlusha, came back. I spoke to the artist when he was doing the mural. The white raven symbolizes good news and birth, and the black ravens represent wisdom."

When they reached the restaurant, it was Kravets who went in first, checking exit routes and sight lines in a single practiced sweep of his head. No, they didn't want a table by the window. Yes, they did want a table against a wall. The staff fussed around Uzeir, treating him like a celebrity—which, Arkady reflected, in this small part of the world was exactly what he was.

The wine was poured: bottles of red and white, both Crimean, INKERMAN on their labels. Food was brought. Arkady hadn't seen anyone make an order.

Uzeir pointed to each dish in turn, rattling off their names as though he were the maître d'. "*Chebureki*, fried meat pasties. *Lagman*, soup with noodles, vegetables, and meat. *Plov*, pilaf with chickpeas and meat. *Churchkhela*, walnuts and raisins dipped in honey and pomegranate juice. *Lepyoshki*, flatbreads. All delicious. This is the best Tatar restaurant you'll find outside of Crimea." He changed the subject without pausing. "So, Arkady, where have your inquiries taken you so far?"

"The Werewolves, mainly."

"The Werewolves? Oh, Leonid wasn't worried about them."

"They're thugs," Elena said.

"Yes, but there's too much showiness about them for him to have taken them seriously. 'Performance art'—that's what he said. You know how it is. It's like a magic trick. The distraction over here catches your eye and draws your attention, so you miss what's going on over there."

Arkady felt hemmed in, without enough room for his elbows when he ate, but when he turned to look at Kravets next to him, he realized that there was plenty of space. A crazed interior designer had set up shop in his head and was playing havoc with his perception, squashing distances in one direction and elongating them in another. The table felt too low, the chair too high. He felt as though he could reach out and touch the far side of the room because his perspective had warped. It had come on out of nowhere and would vanish again just as quickly.

"I'll tell you who Leonid really thought was trouble," Uzeir said.

"Who?"

"Novak."

"Novak?"

"One of Putin's old cronies from his Leningrad days, Konstantin Novak. He's now Crimea's Governor of Sevastopol, and ever since Putin forcefully annexed Crimea from Ukraine in 2014, Novak has been allowed to run Sevastopol as he pleases, so long as it aligns with what Putin wants. It's the line all those powerful men have to walk; do your own thing, but don't get too big for your boots."

"Why exactly did Lebedev think Novak was a threat to him?"

"Novak didn't like that Leonid and I were friends and that we worked together on Forum's plans for the future. The repression against my people in Crimea—that's Novak's doing. He could, if he wanted, make sure the courts behaved fairly and the security forces not overstep their duties. But he doesn't. He chooses not to because it suits Putin."

Even Putin couldn't centralize everything, Arkady thought, so he made sure that he was everywhere in spirit through proxies like Novak. What did Putin want? What did he need? Enemies, the more the better, because only when you had enemies could you justify the terrible things you wanted to do. The Tartars were his enemies, the unwashed, the other.

It came back, Arkady knew, to three things: money, propaganda, and terror. They weren't discrete entities but a triskelion, forever whirling around each other. This was the mindset of spies, the men whose formative years had been spent in the margins of the shadow world. The more rules you break, the more success you have. The game never pauses and never stops. There are no periods of war and peace, just active hostility and retrenchments. There are no threats other than those which can be talked up, or in many cases made up, the better to justify eliminating them. There are no social problems that would be solved if solving them would reduce people's dependence on the state. There are no grand plans, no master strategies, just the lust for power, the insane addictive desire to accumulate more and more because too much is never enough.

Arkady remembered a Soviet-era film in which a king brainwashes his people by using warped mirrors. "It's like the Kingdom of the Crooked Mirrors."

"Exactly. And how do you make those mirrors straight again? I talk to the Western media, for all the good that it does. If no one knows about us, how can anyone help us? Oh, I don't kid myself that it has any more than a small chance of working. But even that's better than nothing. Who do the Western media care about most? Ukraine first, then Crimea, then the Tatars, a third so distant they can hardly see us."

20

It was dark by the time they left the restaurant, the sky stained indigo beyond the streetlights. Arkady was careful how he walked, though the worst of his symptoms had receded. He knew, too, that any unsteadiness he was feeling could be blamed at least in part on the wine. Kravets took the lead, with Elena and Uzeir behind him and Arkady bringing up the rear. He watched father and daughter, and the way their heads almost touched as they conversed.

A trio of teenage girls walked past in gales of laughter, stepping off the pavement and then onto it again to avoid a black Mercedes limousine cruising like a shark through shallows. This could be Paris or Rome, Arkady thought. The air was still warm, the young and the beautiful unafraid. Every city center was a mirage, he knew, whitewashed and historic for the tourists, but now and then it felt good to surrender to the illusion.

Up ahead, a moped weaved its way through slow-moving

traffic toward them. Arkady sensed rather than saw Kravets stiffen and for a moment he wanted to scoff—*Come on, it's just some kid on a moped*—but then people who rode mopeds in city centers on warm nights did so in jeans and T-shirts, not in full leather.

Kravets pulled out his gun but a pistol had already appeared in the rider's hand. Two shots rang out. The report was deafening at such close range.

Kravets pushed Uzeir and Elena down and then covered them with his own body.

The rider gunned his engine and sped away. Kravets regained his feet, his gun aimed at the rider's vanishing back, but there were too many people around for him to get a clean shot, and now Arkady heard the screams and gasps of bystanders.

He dropped to his knees next to Uzeir. Blood stained Uzeir's shirt and oozed in a small pool on the ground. Arkady took off his jacket, opened Uzeir's shirt, and pressed it against the wound in Uzeir's chest.

"It's not too bad," Uzeir said, but his eyes told a different story. Elena was clinging to his hand.

"Quick," Kravets said. "Get him in the car." He had flagged down a passing taxi and opened the rear door.

Arkady put his arms under Uzeir's shoulders while Kravets took his legs. There wasn't much to the old man, but even so, his body felt limp and heavy. Arkady's hands were slick with Uzeir's blood, and he had to adjust his grip to keep hold. Uzeir winced as they put him in the back. Arkady and Elena climbed in alongside him, with Kravets up front.

"I need this like I need teeth in my ass," the driver said. "You'll have to pay for the cleaning, you know."

"Shut the fuck up and drive," Kravets said.

"We'll get you there, Papa." Elena spoke as though talking to a small child.

Uzeir's forehead was covered with sweat and his breath was coming fast and ragged. He closed his eyes, opened them again, and stared at Arkady and Elena as though he was having trouble focusing.

"How long till we get there?" Arkady asked.

"Three minutes," Kravets replied.

Uzeir's eyes had closed again.

"Drive faster!" Arkady shouted.

"I'm getting there as fast as I can, God damn it!" The driver pulled out past a dawdling Fiat and ran a red light. Horns blared; brakes screeched. Arkady saw another car lurch to a stop so suddenly that the driver was thrown forward in his seat.

They pulled up in front of a large building with NATIONAL EMERGENCY AND TRAUMA HOSPITAL above the entrance. Kravets was out of the car before it stopped moving.

"We need help!" he shouted. "Now!"

A couple of paramedics were smoking outside the door. They threw their cigarettes to the side, grabbed a stretcher that was leaning against a wall, and ran over. They moved with confidence, men who had done this a hundred times before and who knew haste was the enemy of speed. They sized up Uzeir's condition, shook the stretcher so the wheels came down, eased him out and onto it, and took him inside.

They waited and fretted. Kravets paced.

Arkady understood. It had been Kravets's responsibility

to keep Uzeir safe. He'd done everything he could. Arkady couldn't fault him.

Elena chewed her nails and silently wept. Arkady knew better than to reassure her. There was a time when he would have tried to say or do something, but now he knew that all she wanted was that he be there beside her.

A steady stream of people came in, the casualties of an average night: a man with a bandage pressed across one eye, a woman in a wheelchair who was breathing with the help of an oxygen tank. Nurses took names and performed basic triage.

A doctor arrived. The white of his coat set off the black rings under his eyes. He addressed Elena as the next of kin.

"First of all, your father's alive."

She pressed her hand to her chest and exhaled.

"There were two bullets. One entered his lower back and punctured his left lung; the other pierced his back, cut through the rib cage and entered the right lung. We think the first bullet has also damaged his spleen, but we can't be sure. We've attached him to an IV, inserted a tube into his rib cage, and drained the air that had seeped into his chest cavity. That brought his pulse back."

"His pulse had stopped?"

"Yes, for a few moments."

"How are his chances?" Arkady asked.

"It's still touch and go. He's lost a lot of blood." He gestured through the main doors, where a crowd had gathered outside. Arkady saw TV cameras. "News of the shooting has gotten out, so you may want to think about what you'd like us to say."

"You mean if he dies?" Elena asked.

"No. I mean generally. Think about it."

134

"I will. Thank you."

The doctor nodded and made a half bow, oddly formal. Elena sighed as she sat down.

"He's alive. That's the main thing."

"Yes," Arkady agreed, but the look he exchanged with Kravets suggested otherwise. He'd seen enough autopsies—and he imagined Kravets had, too—to know that collapsed lungs, damaged spleens, and massive blood loss weren't things which old men simply shook off.

Time passed. Arkady drank coffee from the vending machine and found it to be even worse than the coffee from Petrovka, if that was possible. He had Elena put her head on his lap and try to sleep, but whenever he glanced down her eyes were open.

It was long past midnight when the doctor returned. Arkady knew from the moment he saw him that he had come to deliver bad news, and the only thing more agonizing than the knowledge was having to wait until Elena saw it too.

"No," she said. "No."

"I'm sorry," he said.

"But he was alive."

"His condition rapidly deteriorated. His heart stopped. I tried CPR but he was too frail even for that and he died. I'm so sorry."

Elena was inconsolable. Arkady put his arms around her as she wept.

"First Leonid and now my father. Who's next?" She looked up at him and started crying all over again.

They returned to Uzeir's apartment at three in the morning. Sarah was waiting in the front hall. With tears in her eyes, she tried to comfort her as a mother would a child.

"Is there anything I can get for you?"

Elena shook her head. "Thank you, no."

Speaking softly, Sarah walked her to the bedroom.

"Try to sleep," she said, and, nodding to Arkady, she left.

Both Arkady and Elena collapsed into bed. She slept so deeply that nothing could wake her. He lay awake trying to figure out how the moped driver had known where they would be at that time and what he and Kravets could have done differently.

Five hours later he awoke to find her standing by the window, staring out at the city. Her eyes were dry but sightless. He had seen similar expressions on the faces of loved ones too often during investigations.

"Let's have breakfast," he said.

Sarah had laid out bowls of cereal and a plate of fruit on the kitchen table. Elena poured coffee and sat across from Arkady.

"What do we need to do now?" she asked.

"Go and give evidence to the police. Talk to the press. Deal with the men and women who worked alongside your father here. He was a hero. There must be many."

"There are." She ran her hand through her hair.

Flowers, cards, and candles were placed on the sidewalk where Uzeir had been shot. Elena moved among them, reading each message. Beyond the police cordon, hundreds of Crimean Tatars stood in near silence. Arkady heard some weeping and prayers.

Kravets kept Arkady abreast of the police investigation.

The moped had been found abandoned five blocks away, wiped clean of fingerprints. The owner was a twenty-two-year-old chef who said it had been stolen two nights before, something his friends and colleagues confirmed. Arkady didn't even bother asking whether he'd reported the theft to the police. Might as well tell them you had run out of dish soap. The SBU hadn't received any fresh intelligence of threats to Uzeir or the Crimean Tatar community at large. They were also still looking for connections to the Werewolves, though surely no self-respecting Werewolf would be seen riding such a tiny and unimpressive machine. The Werewolves had chapters in several Russian cities but none in Kyiv for obvious reasons; their brand of aggressive Russian nationalism would not have been welcome.

"I'm guessing it was FSB," Arkady said.

"Of course," Kravets said.

"How many FSB agents are in Kyiv?"

Kravets laughed. "Declared and known agents that we can officially keep tabs on? Very few. But there are also three hundred thousand ethnic Russians living here, so take your pick. How many of those could be trained well enough to fire accurately from a moped? Lots."

"You have informants."

"Yes, but that's no guarantee."

"And the politicians—are they putting pressure on the police to find the killer?"

"Not yet."

This was not a good sign, Arkady thought. He knew he had been spoiled by working for Zurin, whose political machinations were so transparent as to be laughable. Pressure worked in subtle ways: encouragement to pursue an unlikely line of inquiry, a promise to use a certain piece of information wisely, regret that another agency was not pulling its weight the way it should. Bureaucratic inertia could stop even the most determined and idealistic investigator. They never officially or explicitly warned you off, just wore you down until you gave up of your own accord, and then they could turn around and say it had been your choice in the first place.

"I was very fond of him," Kravets continued. "It wasn't an easy task, the one he had. People called it a government-in-exile, and he always laughed at that. He didn't govern anyone, he said. He represented them. It was different."

"He had no power," Arkady said.

"None. And he knew it. He was a symbol. But who wants to be just a symbol? He was an old man. He should have been at home, walking on the promenade in the mornings and playing with his grandchildren in the afternoons. That's what I want when I'm that age. He was thousands of miles from his home, and people looked to him for something he couldn't give."

Who would guess that such a soft heart beat under all that muscle? Arkady patted his shoulder as he said good-bye

★   ★   ★

Back at the apartment, Arkady rang Victor.

"There you are," Victor said.

"Have you been trying to reach me?"

"No."

Arkady laughed. "Thanks. Did you see the news about Uzeir Osmanov?"

"Of course. And I figured you would ring when you could."

"I might have been incapacitated. Dead, even."

"Then you wouldn't have rung." Victor didn't allow emotions to get in the way of logic. "But I'm glad you're okay. How's your girlfriend?"

"As you'd imagine. Badly shaken."

"Tell her I'm sorry."

"I will. What news on the Lebedev investigation?" Victor had taken Arkady's place on the task force.

"Exactly what you'd expect. The Chechens have confessed." He paused. "Poor bastards."

"So that's it?"

"That's it."

"And what reason are they giving for having done this?"

"That they were paid." The cynicism of it, Arkady thought. It was a foolproof method. After waiting a day or two, FSB laid the blame on Chechens to cover up crimes of the state. They couldn't even be bothered to ascribe some fictional ideological motive to them in their fictional confessions. Even in the land of make-believe, they had to be portrayed as filthy mercenaries.

"Now the lawyers are preparing for the trial, to be held both imminently and at a date no one's yet sure of. Sentence first, verdict afterwards." There were few primers on Russian politics more accurate than *Alice's Adventures in Wonderland*.

"And Alex Levin's murder?"

"The same, but without the bullshit confessions."

Ukrainian news showed what Russian news wouldn't: the demonstrations against Uzeir's murder. Crimean Tatars came

139

in the thousands to the city centers: to Lenin Square in Simferopol, to Nakhimov Square in Sevastopol, and to Independence Square in Kyiv. They held up pictures of Uzeir and placards that said, TATARS BELONG HERE! and PUTIN, ARE YOU THE KILLER?

In Moscow, Yashin leaned against his bike and stared down the lens of a TV camera. "The Crimean Tatars were deported in 1944 because they were collaborators and traitors. Now they are protesting against Russia. Soon the Werewolves will be going south to Crimea, as we do every year, and let there be no doubt: when we are there, we will defend ethnic Russians as we always have. We don't go looking for a fight, but we will not shy away from one either. And to the Tatars I say only this: Crimea is no longer your country. If you get in our way, you will be deported again, and this time you will never be allowed back."

He said it in the same reasonable tone of voice he had used with Arkady by the pond in Moscow, but the malevolence below it was so strong that, even here in Ukraine, Elena shuddered.

The footage cut back to Crimea. A man in a suit was standing behind a bank of microphones.

"That's him," Elena said. "That's Novak."

Arkady examined Novak through the screen. A pasty, doughy face, with the beginning of jowls spilling over his collar and eyes deep-set and suspicious. The face of a certain type of Russian. Uzeir had said that Novak came from St. Petersburg, where he was one of Putin's old KGB cronies. They all had that look about them.

The report then cut to St. Petersburg: the briefest establishing shot of the *Bronze Horseman*, and then Arkady was shocked to see Tatiana holding a microphone. *TATIANA PETROVNA*, NEW YORK TIMES *CORRESPONDENT*, said the caption. A breeze ruffled her hair as she spoke. "I had the privilege of speaking with Uzeir Osmanov several times over the past months. He was an eloquent and passionate advocate for the Crimean Tatar men and women who have been forgotten for too long."

He looked away from the screen. If Elena hadn't been there, he would have changed the channel. He was shocked to see her so suddenly, still out there, still telling the truth. Would she have had the same reaction if she saw him suddenly on her television? That was always the great unknown when someone had gone, because gone didn't necessarily mean forgotten. At the very least, Arkady thought, he wanted Tatiana to remember him. All this went through his mind in a flash, and on top of it came an equally sudden surge of guilt. He was here with Elena, who needed his support, and he shouldn't be agonizing over a woman who had walked out on him.

"That's her!" Elena exclaimed. "That's her!"

For a moment Arkady thought Elena was talking about Tatiana, and he wondered how she was able to recognize her, but when he looked at the screen again, Tatiana was gone and the camera was back on Novak. There were three people standing behind him as he spoke, two men and a woman. Arkady looked closer and saw who the woman was a split second before Elena said it out loud.

"Karina."

She didn't want to speculate about what Karina was doing there with Novak, the man responsible for cracking down on the Tatars in Sevastopol. Karina had supported the Tatar cause when she worked for Forum, and it wasn't that Karina had just been standing there by chance, caught in the crowd. She was right behind Novak, the place where the trusted ones got to stand and look solemnly supportive.

"We have to go to Crimea if we want to find her," Arkady said.

SEVASTOPOL

21

They drove in shifts as before. The air grew warmer, and Arkady didn't need a map to know they were traveling south. He was a medieval mapmaker contemplating the way land fell away to the water, a migrating bird navigating by some magnetic orientation he could not explain.

They changed places at the wheel four hours later.

"She was something to you, wasn't she?"

She phrased it so casually that it took a moment to realize who she was talking about.

"Tatiana?"

"I saw your reaction when she appeared."

"It was a shock, that's all."

"No. It was a shock, but that's not all. Tell me."

"Why?"

"Because I want to know."

"Why do you want to know?"

145

"Because she's important to you."

He told her how he had first heard Tatiana's voice on tape recordings and chased her halfway across Siberia before finding her hiding out in Kaliningrad. When he finished, he felt so empty that he asked her to pull over so he could get some air.

"Thank you," she said when he got back in the car. "What I really want to know is are you still in love with her?"

"I don't know. All I can say is that I'm happy with you now. How about you? You must have had someone important to you."

Then she told him of the men in her life. There had been several boyfriends over the years but only one that she'd really loved. He was called Rustem, a Moscow lawyer. Smart, serious, cerebral, and idealistic. Socially, he could be shy and was often happy to sit in silence for hours at a time, but at work or in court he was totally transformed, by turns passionate, infuriatingly accurate in his arguments, and funny when he needed to be. He had defended many of his fellow Tatars, challenging the prosecutors on obscure points of law, and forcing them to resubmit documents and delay trials. His clients still went to jail, of course, because that was the way the system was rigged, but their sentences were lighter than they would have been without Rustem.

What did the authorities do when they couldn't outwit Rustem? They arrested him and handed him over to Center E, a department tasked with fighting "extremist activity and terrorism." They charged him with offenses under code 280, extremism, and code 282, separatism. He knew the law better than they did. They didn't care. They wouldn't let Elena come to see him in custody, nor would they let his parents or his brother and sister. And three weeks after arresting him they dumped his body on the side of a road outside Sevastopol and said he'd been shot while trying to escape during an administrative transfer.

It hadn't made her give up on love, or hope, or her belief in things that were right. Nor was it anything as simplistic as wanting to do good in Rustem's memory. He of all people would have hated that—would have hated the sentimentality behind it.

"Now that Uzeir is dead, I intend to help the Tatars. There will always be something I can do for them."

So much of Elena reminded him of Tatiana. She refused to accept injustice but, unlike Tatiana, she didn't let injustice consume her.

It took them four hours to clear the border into Crimea at Kalanchak. The Ukrainians let them out without a problem, but the Russians on the Crimean border checked Elena's papers, called Moscow, and were told that Uzeir Osmanov's daughter could be trouble. Arkady and Elena were separated and then brought back into the same room. Men appeared and vanished. Elena snapped.

"You know who I am," she said. "I have never been accused of any crime, let alone convicted of one. My papers are all in order."

Finally, phone calls were made to Moscow, where Zurin's authority gave them the needed permission.

An officer walked back with them to the car and raised the gate himself to let them pass through. Arkady saw that a car was waiting just beyond the barrier and pulled out behind them as they passed. It was three and a half hours to Sevastopol, the capital. The car tracked them all the way.

22

Arkady looked out across the harbor. A speedboat zipped between gray ranks of warships, churning up a wake that spent itself uselessly on the vast hulls of the destroyers and frigates. This was the Black Sea Fleet, not hidden away and cordoned off but sharing the bay with passenger boats and leisure craft. Arkady wondered how easy it would be for an enterprising terrorist to attach a limpet mine to one of those hulls. There had to be more security than there seemed to be.

He and Elena had been waiting almost an hour. The governor's offices were down on the waterfront, and Elena wanted to catch Karina by surprise, so they had taken up position on a bench across the road from the main entrance. It was twelve-thirty. Chances were that Karina would come out sooner or later for lunch. Of course, she might not even be working in this building, but if she'd been so close to Novak in the TV footage, then presumably she wouldn't be too far from where he was.

Elena sat very still. She kept her gaze trained on the building, as though through sheer force of will she could drag Karina outside.

"You don't mind?" she asked.

"Not at all." Arkady was used to waiting. Most of an investigator's life was waiting, one way or another.

A small snake slithered over the grass in front of them. Elena didn't see it. It had a black nose with delicate red markings toward the tail. It's head was triangular in shape, a sign that it was venomous. Arkady held his breath until it disappeared. This was a more entertaining stakeout than usual. Or had that been a hallucination?

"If you want to go . . ."

"I don't."

He wondered whether this was something that Elena should do alone. One friend's betrayal of another was so personal that any explanation should come just between the two of them, but Elena had asked him to be there, perhaps for fear that she would forget to say what she needed to say, and in any case Arkady had promised Bronson that he would find Karina.

"If you want me to leave at any point, just let me know," he said.

"You're just worried it's going to get emotional," she laughed.

"Could be."

Downtown Sevastopol was a peninsula, just like Crimea itself was a peninsula within a peninsula. It was bounded by the inlets of South Bay and Artillery Bay, and its buildings boasted Venetian arches and columned balconies. Here was where families came every summer evening for a promenade, strolling along avenues and boulevards, breathing in the sea air, stopping to speak with people they knew, or simply smiling at others who also had the good fortune to have ended up here rather than in one of Russia's many small, grim towns.

"There," Elena said softly.

Arkady looked. Karina was coming out of the building, chatting with another woman. She swept her sunglasses down from the top of her head as she stepped into the light and hitched her handbag a little higher on her shoulder.

Elena started moving, quickening her pace to step between passing cars as she crossed the road. Arkady followed.

"Karina!" Elena's voice was loud and firm. Karina looked around, momentarily confused, trying to see where the call had come from.

"Here!" This time Karina saw her, and the shock seemed to stop her dead. She stood stock-still staring at Elena, then she said something to the woman next to her, who nodded and walked away.

"What a surprise!" Karina said as she approached Elena.

"I bet it is."

Karina stopped a few feet from her, unsure whether she dared reach out and hug Elena. Elena didn't make it easy for her. She stood without a smile.

"This is Arkady Renko of the Moscow prosecutor's office," Elena said.

Arkady stepped forward and shook her hand. "Your father asked me to find you. It hasn't been easy."

Karina ran her hand through her hair. "I can explain."

"Can you?" Elena asked.

"I can." She paused. "Well, I can try."

She took them to a café three blocks away, far enough from the office not to run into anyone she knew. They settled in a booth with benches on either side of the table, Karina on one side, Elena and Arkady on the other. Arkady signaled for the waiter to bring three glasses and a bottle of wine. He filled the glasses and handed one to her. She nodded gratefully.

"I turned myself inside and out trying to figure out how to tell you, but I couldn't so I did the one thing I shouldn't have done: nothing. I took the coward's way out and left without a word. I'm sorry."

"But why? I don't get it. People were worried sick about you."

"I know."

"You could just have texted to say you were okay."

"I know that too. But the longer I was gone, the harder it was to talk to you."

"Alex was murdered. Leonid too."

"I saw. It's just so awful."

"'Just so awful'? That's it?" Elena was furious. "You were part of it—part of the cause. You were senior, you were trusted. Alex would have done anything for you. Leonid was someone you loved and looked up to."

"What else do you want me to say?"

"The truth. Why you left, why you came back here. You owe me that at least."

Karina puffed her cheeks and blew out. She looked at Arkady. He kept his expression neutral.

"I left because I was disillusioned with Forum."

"You mean you were scared."

"No. I was disillusioned."

"You stopped believing in the cause?"

"No. I always believed in the cause. I still do."

"Then why?"

"I didn't believe we were getting anywhere. All the work we put in and no effective outcome."

"How can you say that? We had protests, rallies, and media coverage. Our people have been killed. If we didn't have an effect, why would they go to such lengths?"

"They kill people because they can," Karina said. "Yes, we had rallies, and people turned up, but it was a drop in the ocean."

"It's a drop in the ocean at the moment. But it will build."

"Everyone who's gone up against Putin has thought that. And guess what? He's still there, and they're either dead or exiled."

There wasn't much arguing with that, Arkady thought.

"Okay, say that you're right—which I'm not—but, for the sake of argument, why come back here to work for a man who you know has it in for the Tatars? Why not do something else? *Anything* else?"

"Because I was tired of Moscow. I know this place. It's my home and I love it. I was offered a job as Konstantin Novak's assistant because they'd seen what I'd been doing at Forum."

Elena's laugh was devoid of mirth. "And his policies toward the Tatars?"

"I hope that in time I can persuade him to go easier there."

"*Persuade* him? You're his assistant, right?"

"Right."

"Regional governors don't take policy advice from their assistants."

153

"Maybe he'll be the first."

"You don't believe Forum will make a difference, but you believe *you* can? Do you have any idea how delusional that sounds?"

"I can't make you understand."

"You're right about that. I need some fresh air," Elena said.

She stood up, banging her knee on the underside of the table. Arkady slid out of the booth to let her past. He saw that she was trying not to cry. He sat back down.

"Do you have the same number your father has for you?"

"Yes."

"I have that, too, but can you write down your address so I can tell him where you are?"

"I'd rather not. He'll send some of his goons down to bring me back to Moscow. I don't even want him to know I'm in Crimea. Listen, you don't have to call him. I'll call him. I'll tell him that you found me and not to worry. I'm okay."

"He's my client. I have to talk to him. Let me give you my number just in case. I don't know what you're doing with Novak, but I hope you realize he's a dangerous man."

Arkady left Karina and found his car. Elena was waiting in it. She had obviously been crying. He put his arm around her and drew her close. There was nothing he could say.

He started the car and drove a few miles from the center of Sevastopol to Inkerman, where Elena had found them an apartment online. From the window, he could see the mouth of the Chorna River where it entered the bay, and beyond that he saw the warships he'd seen earlier.

He remembered that there had been a battle here in Inkerman back in the nineteenth century when Russia was fighting the British, the French, and the Ottomans. Perhaps he had been taught it at school, though—given that Russia had lost that particular war—he doubted it. He didn't remember much else about the battle except that it had been fought in fog so thick that troops on both sides had been cut off from each other, and so they had been obliged to fight on their own initiative rather than according to orders from their commanders. It became known as the "Soldiers' Battle," the one pitched event of the entire campaign when the rank and file were left to their own devices and won.

That was how Arkady felt now: that he was battling through fog. Not just that he'd been left to his own devices—Zurin had pretty much cut him loose from the start—but that Arkady's only connection with the office in Moscow was checking in with Victor every now and then.

By this stage he usually had some idea of what was going on and who was responsible, and from there it was simply a matter of finding enough evidence to bring charges that would stick. But here he had no idea. He didn't even know what he didn't know, and that scared him.

23

Bronson caught the first flight down from Moscow and demanded that Arkady take him to see Karina.

"I have to," Arkady told Elena. "He's one of the reasons I'm here."

"Fine," Elena said. "Just as long as I don't have to see her."

Arkady took a taxi out to the airport. He saw Bronson from halfway across the arrivals area. Bronson seemed oblivious to the way people were staring at him, though maybe, if you looked like Bronson, you were so used to people staring at you, it became the norm.

He embraced Arkady and asked him questions all the way into town. How had Arkady known Karina was here? What reasons did she give for her disappearance? How did she seem to him? Arkady answered as fully as he could but skirted around anything to do with Elena.

"I knew I could count on you." Bronson beamed.

"Like I said, it was luck. I saw her on TV. Total chance."

"Ukrainian TV, not Russian TV. Which you'd never have seen unless you'd been in Kyiv to start with. You say it was luck, but you know and I know there's no such thing."

Arkady didn't feel like getting into a semantic discussion.

The taxi dropped them right outside the governor's office. Two security men moved swiftly to head Bronson off as he walked in. He looked as though he could sweep up one in each arm and crack their skulls without breaking stride, but he stopped and smiled at them, which was in some ways even more terrifying.

"I'm here to see my daughter," Bronson said.

His name was taken, a call was made upstairs, and Bronson and Arkady were asked to wait on chairs by a window. The security guard kept a nervous eye on Bronson, as though he might turn on him at any moment. Again Bronson seemed not to notice.

Karina came downstairs five minutes later. Bronson was on his feet the moment he saw her, and he embraced her with the same ferocity as he'd embraced Arkady but with substantially more tenderness.

"Why didn't you call me?" he asked.

"It's a long story," she said.

The three of them walked outside onto the government grounds. Arkady sat down on a bench as father and daughter wandered off, talking. They were too far away to hear, but Arkady saw Bronson wipe away tears once or twice.

Finally, they came over to Arkady.

"Thank you for returning my daughter to me," he said to Arkady. "Not that she will come home."

"Father's going back to the hotel for a rest, but could I talk with you?"

"Of course."

She turned to Bronson. "Father, I'll meet you at your hotel, and after you nap, I'll take you to a good Crimean restaurant."

She waited until Bronson found a taxi before speaking.

"How much did you tell him?" she asked.

"What I felt it my business to tell him. No more."

"Do you have time for lunch?"

She took him back to the same café as before.

"You have to have the borscht," she said. "On a summer day, there's nothing like it. Russian borscht, of course. I've come to prefer Russian food in general."

"What's the difference?"

"Russians cook with beef, fish, and chicken. Ukrainians rely on pork and goose for their meat. That's why it's so fatty and heavy."

Two bowls of borscht appeared.

"Khrushchev liked to say that the best chicken in Ukraine was pork sausage."

Arkady laughed. "So what do you want to talk to me about?"

"You don't presume this is a date?" He saw mockery beneath the amusement. "I'm teasing you. I saw the way you are with Elena."

"She's having a hard time at the moment."

"She knows you're here?"

"She knows I was bringing your father to see you, yes."

"Good. Because I lied to you both yesterday, and I don't want there to be any more lies."

"You're going to tell me the truth?"

"Yes."

"Don't you think it would be better if Elena were here too?"

"I'd rather tell you and then you can tell her. She's not happy with me at the moment. I don't want you involved; on the other hand, I want her to know that I didn't just walk out and betray her and that there are good reasons for doing what I'm doing."

Arkady was used to the way people talked around difficult subjects before finally getting there.

"You have to promise to only tell Elena."

"Who else am I going to tell?"

"My father, for one."

"Your father asked me to find you, nothing more. But three people have been murdered since your father hired me. If what you've got to tell me has anything to do with those murders, I'll use that information. Otherwise, I promise only to tell Elena."

She took a deep breath. "I didn't go to work for Novak because I wanted to. It was Leonid's idea. He heard a job vacancy had just turned up there and he encouraged me to apply. He couldn't write me a recommendation, of course, because Novak would have been suspicious right away. But he called in some favors, friends from the old days. That got me in the door."

"Why did he want you to work there?"

"Novak is an ally of Putin's. He's a powerful man and, like all of Putin's friends, he's rich. Leonid wanted me to find ways to discredit him. He knew it wasn't enough just to proclaim Forum the future. He needed to discredit the opposition."

"How did he expect to do it?"

"He wanted me to uncover something criminal that Novak

had been up to. Something really criminal, something which would compromise him when it came out."

"Such as what?"

"Leonid thought that Novak might have stolen money from the government to build a yacht for himself that cost over a billion rubles."

"So, have you found anything?"

"Yes, but they may lead nowhere, and I don't think I can risk taking documents out of the building."

"You're sure no one there knows who you are?"

"Yes."

"How?"

"I've worked and lived thousands of miles away, and even when I was there, nobody even knew what I was doing for Leonid. They just thought I was his girlfriend."

"Were you?"

"Yes."

"Then it must have been a terrible shock for you when he was killed. You never let on?"

"Never. I cried my eyes out every morning before I left home and every night when I came back. When Novak said we should celebrate Leonid's death, I plastered on a smile and raised my glass."

"Who else in Forum knows about what you're doing?"

"No one. Just me, now that Leonid is dead."

"No one at all?"

"No one at all. No paper trail or electronic traces either. It was an idea we discussed in person and only ever in person. Leonid said we had to compartmentalize. 'We're at war,' he said. 'We have to act that way.'"

"What I don't understand is why Novak would employ someone who was open about the fact she had been working for a party opposed to his own."

"Because I told him what I told Elena and you yesterday: that I'd become disillusioned with it and that I wanted to come back home."

"And?"

"And what?"

Arkady tipped his bowl over to one side and spooned out the last of the borscht. He heard her sigh.

"Okay. And Novak does business with my father."

Arkady wondered if he could believe any of what she had just told him. If it was true, she should have told Elena in the first place. Was it that she just needed time to come up with a better story?

★ ★ ★

Arkady found Elena in an assembly hall with a few dozen Crimean Tatars. They had asked her there so they could share their grief with her but also to ask that she continue Uzeir's fight.

The leader of the group was an old Tatar wearing a traditional embroidered cap and cummerbund.

"We're here to honor Uzeir Osmanov, who was killed on the streets of Kyiv one week ago today. He lived to the age of eighty-three and, as you know, spent most of his life striving to return the Tatars to their homeland here in Crimea. The one place he wanted to live, and was not allowed to live, was

Crimea. That's all Uzeir wanted, a home—*our* home. Today we have Uzeir's daughter, Elena, with us."

Elena stood up and walked to the front of the hall.

"I have trouble finding the words to describe how I feel about my father's death. I'm better at expressing myself with music, so I would like to play Bach's Adagio in G Minor for you."

She tucked her violin under her chin, raised her bow to the strings, and played with such purity and sadness that tears came to the eyes of everyone who listened.

★　★　★

There was an unmarked car outside the assembly hall. Arkady tipped an imaginary hat at the driver, who scowled.

"Are they bothering you?" he asked as they left the hall.

"No. If anything, I find it reassuring."

"How?"

"It means that at least they're where I can see them."

It was logic, Arkady conceded. Russian logic, of course, but then, Crimea was Russian now.

He drove her back to the apartment in Inkerman. He wanted to tell her what Karina had told him, but he didn't trust the FSB not to have bugged his car. He parked, and as they walked to their apartment building, he told her what Karina had said. She stepped back to see his face.

"You believe her?" Elena asked.

"I don't know."

24

It was easier than Arkady had thought to get to see Novak. He
sent the request through Karina herself, as would have been
the case even if he'd had no connection to her.

> I am Arkady Renko, investigator with the Moscow police.
> I am working on the case of Uzeir Osmanov and would
> appreciate the opportunity to talk with you.

The reply came back within the hour.

> I am not sure how much help I can give you but would of
> course be delighted to assist in any way possible.

The phrasing, Arkady noted, was almost identical to that of
Yashin. He wondered whether his inquiries with Novak would
be similarly fruitless.

They emailed back and forth on possible times for the interview. Arkady, of course, had no pressing commitments, but Novak could spare only a few minutes here and there in between meetings. Eventually, Novak had come back with something Arkady hadn't been expecting: *I have to take a trip tomorrow out to the east of the peninsula, and if you are amenable, we can talk in the car. It will take most of the day there and back, so I understand if this is a time commitment you can't afford, but you would be most welcome.*

Yes, Arkady had replied, that would be fine—and now here he was, settling into the back of a black Mercedes limousine with Novak alongside him and a chauffeur up front.

"You don't mind if my assistant tags along?" Novak asked.

"Of course not," Arkady said, nodding toward Karina as though they'd never met.

Karina sat up front with the chauffeur, and Arkady pulled the glass screen across so that he and Novak could talk in private. If Karina could listen, then there was a chance she could say or do something to give herself away—a remote chance, sure, but she was untrained, and Arkady wanted to keep variables to a minimum. Besides, Novak would expect Arkady to close the screen: walls, and employees, had ears.

Novak gestured to a small mahogany cupboard in front of them. "Wine, champagne, vodka. Please, help yourself."

"Thank you, no." Arkady was conscious of the shabbiness of his clothes against the white leather seats. He couldn't remember the last time he had been in something so luxurious. The air-conditioning made him shiver, and the double glazing on the windows was so clear that the world outside passed by like a silent film.

"So," Novak said, "Uzeir Osmanov. Terrible business. I hope the investigation is close to finding the guilty party, though of course I understand that you're limited in what you can tell me."

"Yes, but limited also in the sense that it is the Kyiv authorities taking the lead. I was there as part of inquiries into the murder of Leonid Lebedev."

"Another terrible business. I know it's a risk that all of us in the political arena have to accept as the price for public service, but still it's always a tragedy when it happens."

"Did you know Uzeir Osmanov?"

"Of course. I met with him several times over the years before he left for Kyiv."

"And how did you find him?"

"On a personal level, I liked him very much. On a political level, we had our differences, as you would expect."

"He says he left for his own safety."

"Then that was his choice. To the best of my knowledge, he was never threatened, let alone arrested—certainly not by anyone in an official capacity. Perhaps he had some unsavory encounters with local thugs. We have a small element of those, regrettably, just as every city does."

"He said that you had encouraged a crackdown on the Crimean Tatars here."

"I have instructed law enforcement to perform their duties. There are many members of the Crimean Tatar community who belong to banned Islamic extremist organizations. Would you rather I turned a blind eye to that?"

"He said that those charges are all trumped-up and that innocent men can spend twenty years in jail for something they didn't do."

"If you have specifics from any of these cases, I would be happy to have them investigated and check that proper oversight was followed. Islamic extremist terrorism is the scourge of many countries, and unfortunately we are no exception. Crimea is an integral part of Russia, and I make no apologies for standing firm against any and all those who would try to undermine that."

"In other words, you take your orders from Moscow."

"I adhere to the law. I can assure you, Investigator, that I'm nobody's poodle, nor is anyone else in Sevastopol. This has always been a city which marches to the beat of its own drum."

It was like trying to trap an eel and always losing his grip. Novak proclaimed his commitment to the law and his pride in Crimea, Arkady tried to get through the bland political answers to the grit beneath. It was an easy, cheap, and not altogether accurate accusation to make, that all politicians were criminals, but they certainly knew their way around a lie, and more to the point around lying as a default policy when answering even innocuous questions. Why had Novak invited him to spend most of the day here if he was going to be so uncooperative? They could have done this in one of those snatches of minutes between meetings.

Arkady gave up, or rather he let the conversation drift on to other matters, hoping that he could return to the topic later and perhaps catch Novak with his defenses down.

Novak passed the rest of the journey expounding on the virtues of Crimea as though he were a medieval potentate showing Arkady around his personal estate. It was a diamond, a teardrop hanging suspended from the mainland by the thinnest of isthmuses, and to look at it on the map was to believe that one day it could just fall away forever into a warm maritime embrace. Its coasts traced curves so voluptuous, an Armenian woman would have been proud of them. They were on the same latitude as the South of France here, did Arkady know that? This was where Romanov tsars and Politburo bigwigs had come. It was the playground of the rich and famous and always had been, even when being rich and famous had been officially frowned upon. Novak pointed at orchards whose trees groaned beneath the weight of apricots and peaches, at vineyards marching across fields in even ranks, at small coastal villages nestling in the lee of cliffs.

The sea, which had been on their right all journey long, now seemed to swing around until it was straight in front of them. Arkady saw two slivers stretching across the water all the way to the horizon that were a road bridge and a rail bridge side by side, thin strips of engineering genius standing proud and vulnerable against the vastness of the water.

There was a turnout just before the bridge began. The chauffeur pulled over, parked, and came around to open Novak's door. The air was warm after the air-conditioning. Arkady stretched his legs and back, uncoiling. Karina smiled at him.

Novak gestured across the water. "The Kerch Strait. Here, Crimea. There, Russia. In between, the Kerch Bridge. Eighteen kilometers, two billion dollars, three years. Built by my companies under my personal supervision. We had to deal with tectonic faults, mud volcanoes, and thick layers of silt. I found the best engineers in the world. The president himself laid the first pillar at the beginning of construction and came to open it at the end, driving the very first truck across. Free of charge to drivers in both directions."

"Impressive," Arkady said.

Novak looked at him, perhaps seeking evidence of sarcasm, but Arkady was perfectly serious. As a young boy he'd been enamored of their beauty and fascinated by the engineering it took to build them. That fascination had never completely left him, and so it was that he could stand here, look out across the strait, and feel that Novak had earned his right to boast.

"You're wondering why we've come all the way out here, aren't you?"

"As a matter of fact, I was. A bridge inspection?"

"Not as such."

"Then what?"

"Be patient." He looked at his watch. "It won't be long."

A TV van pulled up behind them. Arkady saw a camera crew get out. Karina went over and spoke to them. Arkady saw nods, gestures, checking of angles.

The chauffeur ducked back inside the car and returned with a pair of binoculars. Novak took them, looked through them, smiled, and handed them to Arkady.

"Look."

Arkady raised them to his eyes. It took him a moment to focus them so that the image was sharp. Even with the magnification and foreshortening, it was a sight which made him catch his breath. There were hundreds of them, and even at two or three abreast the line must have stretched a mile or more. People called them a gang, but they seemed more like an invading force, a militia from somewhere beyond the wastelands, engines snarling, deep and malevolent, and Yashin riding one-handed at the front.

The Werewolves blocked the bridge for a good half hour while Novak welcomed them all to the Crimea. He hugged Yashin, posed for photos with him, gave an interview to the obliging TV cameraman. Arkady watched while traffic built up behind the motorcycles, but no one dared remonstrate or even honk. Biker gangs were intimidating at the best of times, even when they weren't explicitly backed by the Kremlin.

Arkady found the whole thing excruciating.

Then the Werewolves were riding in convoy all the way to Sevastopol, with Novak's Mercedes in the middle of them. Arkady watched as motorcycles came past and dropped back, the strangely graceful ballet of machines maneuvering around each other.

"I used to be a biker myself, you know," Novak said, and beneath the smooth politician's exterior Arkady saw a man who still fancied himself the easy rider outlaw of legend.

Arkady saw people on the streets as they approached Sevastopol, some who had clearly heard that the convoy was coming and had been waiting to see it, others who'd been taken by surprise and shied from its sound and fury. A small child clapped his hands over his ears and ran screaming into his house as though fleeing a monster, a vast metallic dragon roaring and belching smoke as it rushed past.

It was late afternoon by the time they arrived back in Nakhimov Square. The crowd there was in the hundreds, and the Werewolves were quick to form concentric circles around Yashin with their bikes, just as Arkady had seen them do at Sparrow Hills, and to let members of the public in only one or two at a time. Yashin posed for selfies, hugged babushkas, hoisted babies up on his one arm. Arkady heard cooing and gasps alike, from women who wanted to mother Yashin and those who wanted to seduce him.

A stage had been erected at the foot of the statue to Admiral Nakhimov himself. Yashin climbed the steps. Novak was there already, wearing his best shit-eating grin. The men embraced again, and Novak handed Yashin a microphone.

"We came here in 2014," Yashin said, and the crowd cheered. "We came here in 2014 to restore this beautiful place, this special place, to its rightful status. It was a tectonic shift for Russia. For the first time we showed resistance to the growing savagery of the West, the rush to consumerism that denies all spirituality, the destruction of traditional values, and the threat of American democracy.

"Sevastopol has long occupied a treasured place in the Russian hearts and minds and will always do so. It is both our honor and our responsibility to be here for Mother Russia."

The crowd roared. Arkady knew there was a thin line between standing up for one's beliefs and being swept up in other people's madness—knew, too, that the line was drawn differently, depending on who you were. He wondered where his own line was and how close all this came to crossing it.

"Impressive? Scary? A bit of both?"

He recognized the voice in his ear immediately, and as ever it was as though she had plucked the thoughts straight from his head. When he turned to look at her, her eyes carried the same challenge they always had, her mouth the same flicker of amusement.

"Tatiana," he said.

25

If it had been a shock seeing her on TV, it was nothing compared to seeing her in the flesh. He was struck again by her gray-green eyes and her smile full of humor. When Arkady spoke, the words were inept, and while it was a warm evening, it had nothing to do with the heat he felt. A man thinks he is over a lover, that she is only a distant memory, and then she appears out of nowhere and he feels only an unfathomable sense of loss.

"It's no less of a shock for me," she said when they had found a side street.

"Probably more," Arkady said. "I saw you on TV the other day, talking about Uzeir Osmanov. I should have realized you would be here."

"Wherever the story is."

"And the story is . . . ?"

"The mood among the Crimean Tatars following Uzeir's

175

murder and what it has to do with Putin's Angels coming down here. And you? Why are you here?"

In a few words, he told her what had been happening since he left Russia.

"Are you in love with her?" she asked.

"I'm with her."

"That's not what I asked."

"That's the only answer you're going to get."

"I'd like to meet her."

"Why?"

"Curiosity."

"You don't get right of approval, you know."

"No?"

She put her hand on his forearm. "We have to talk about it—not right now, but sometime."

"What's there to say? You had enough. You left."

"For an investigator, you have no understanding of human nature."

She knew how to get to him.

"Also, as an investigator, you never asked the right question."

"Which was . . . ?"

"Was there anything you could have done to make me change my mind?"

"I knew there wasn't."

"No. You assumed there wasn't."

"If I'd asked you that, what would you have said?"

"It doesn't matter what I'd have said."

"It does."

"No, it doesn't. What matters is that, had I said something, then it would have been up to you to decide whether you were prepared to accept it."

Arkady reflected that he had rarely won an argument with Tatiana.

"Perhaps we can help each other," he said. "Professionally."

"Nice dodge."

"It's all I've got right now."

"Okay, professionally, what do you have for me?"

"At the moment, not much. But I'm looking for a murderer, you're looking for a story. If we find something that might be of interest to the other, it would be helpful to share, right?"

"Thesis plus antithesis equals synthesis?"

He laughed. "Spoken like a true Soviet."

"Originally Hegel, though."

"Logical."

Her turn to laugh.

"You have my number?" she asked.

"Not anymore. I had to resist the temptation to get in touch with you."

"Clearly, it worked. Here, let me give you my number again."

"No need."

"Oh?"

"I can still remember it."

She smiled. "How annoying for you."

"Very."

Karina and Elena had agreed to meet for breakfast at a waterfront café. Arkady drove Elena down there, and, as always, the FSB followed.

"You should take those guys on a car chase," Elena said. "Give them something to do." She raised her voice. "Flash your lights if you can hear me, gentlemen."

Arkady glanced in the rearview mirror. Their lights didn't flash.

"No bug here or no sense of humor there," Elena concluded.

"The two are not necessarily mutually exclusive." He stopped in front of the café.

"That's true." She kissed him.

Arkady watched her go into the café before checking his mirrors and pulling out into the traffic. The FSB car didn't follow him. Their orders were to stay only on Elena. He would find a café of his own, take a coffee in the morning sun, and phone Victor.

A traffic light was turning red up ahead. If Arkady hit the gas, he could probably just about make it in time, but it was a beautiful morning and he had nowhere particular to be, so he coasted gently to a stop and waited. On his right, he saw a pedestrian area leading down to the shore.

Two men were arguing—not a full-blown argument, perhaps, but certainly a heated discussion. The one on the left was chopping the air with his hands, and whatever point he was making, it was clear that he was unhappy and agitated. The one on the right was making placating gestures—which was ironic, Arkady thought, as the man on the right was Bronson, and he could have snapped Novak's neck in a heartbeat.

There was a free parking space up ahead. Arkady slid his car into it and got out. Novak wagged his finger at Bronson and turned away. Arkady saw his Mercedes idling at the curb. The chauffeur got out to open the door.

Bronson pulled out his mobile phone, stabbed at the screen, and held it to his ear. He saw Arkady walking up the path and gestured to the phone. Arkady shrugged and sat down on a nearby bench. Bronson didn't look especially happy, but Arkady didn't care.

"Call me back," Bronson barked into the phone, and ended the call with another violent stab of a meaty finger. He turned to Arkady. "Now's not an especially good time."

"It is for me." Arkady pointed at the departing Mercedes. "What was all that about?"

"Mind your own business."

"I'm minding yours."

"This is nothing to do with you."

"Isn't it? Let's see. You ask me to find your daughter, which I did. It turns out that she's working for an old friend of yours. It also turns out that three people with connections to her have been murdered since you sent me on this chase—without payment, if you recall."

"I offered to pay."

"You did, that's true. And now I'd like to take you up on that. Not with money but with information. What were you arguing about?"

"I promise you, this has nothing to do with your investigation."

"Then tell me and I'll know for sure."

Bronson sighed. "All right." He pointed out into the bay. "You see over there?"

Arkady followed the direction of Bronson's finger. "Where am I looking?"

"Over there. Yes, that's it." Arkady saw a swimmer, a naval frogman, by the look of it, with a mask and scuba gear. "Now wait a moment."

The surface of the water was suddenly broken by a dolphin. It leapt high, twisting itself in the air so that water droplets flew in all directions, catching the sun, then it dove back under the water and began to swim fast toward the frogman. The frogman began to swim off to the side, but the dolphin simply adjusted its course to head him off. When it reached the frogman, it lifted its head and brought it down on top of the man's, not hard enough to hurt, but enough to stop him in his tracks. The frogman turned and tried to get past another way, but the dolphin simply went with him and gave him a couple more glancing blows for good measure. An inflatable boat approached and hauled the frogman on board, but the dolphin still wasn't letting them past. It bumped the boat hard, and though the inflatable could have gone past if it really wanted to, the pilot spun the boat in a wide 180 and headed in the other direction.

"Naval dolphins," Bronson said. "Half a dozen of them in all, owned and trained by the Black Sea Fleet. They're amazing in what they can do. Find military frogmen and neutralize them, like you just saw, and they can also carry explosives and detect mines. They're quicker than any man in the water—and probably a lot smarter too. The only problem with them is that if a male dolphin sees a female dolphin during the mating season, he instantly sets off after her. He won't obey any commands; he's totally uncontrollable."

"This sounds like a joke."

Bronson laughed. "Right. But unlike most Russian men, they always come back. Usually after a week or so."

"So what's your interest in the dolphins?"

"Dolphins are expensive and the navy's strapped for cash. I suggested that we expand the city's aquarium and move the dolphins there. The navy could still use them on a part-time basis, but they'd be earning money most of the time."

"Money for you."

"I offered to facilitate the deal."

"For a percentage."

"Naturally. Oh—there'd also be a rehabilitation center for disabled children."

"You're all heart."

Animals should live where nature intended, Arkady thought. A dolphin that wanted to chase its mate should be able to do just that, not disable mines or perform tricks for the public or do anything dreamt up by man for his own amusement. He sensed, though, that this was not the time to lecture Bronson.

"So, what's the problem?" he continued.

"Novak's the problem."

"How?"

"I've worked with him for years. I've got interests all the way up and down this Crimean coast. Casinos, bars, hotels, and restaurants."

The way Bronson told it, he was the man who brought in the tourists. Arkady knew that these "interests" were a fraction of what Bronson would like people to think they were. A protection racket here, a small investment there. A lot of small things all added up, but there were hundreds of sharks operating in these waters, all of them hustling for their space just like Bronson was, and there was nothing that made him special among them.

"Yes."

"And we've always had an agreement, Novak and I. He lets me operate the way I like, as long as I give him what he needs."

"Which is . . . ?"

"Running my side of things without causing problems."

"And making money for him."

"Every business has to pay tax."

"To the governor personally?" Arkady asked.

"I pay what we've agreed to. How much goes to him and how much to the city government is not my problem."

"And now he's changing the terms?"

"Yes. Not just with me. With everybody. All done with contracts and lawyers, of course. We're all respectable businessmen now."

Arkady knew that the important word there was "now." In the nineties, the criminals down here had worn shell suits in all colors of the rainbow and neck chains so thick you could have locked bicycles up with them. The peninsula was called the Ukrainian Sicily, and it wasn't meant as a compliment. Of course, most of the bandits ended up either dead or in jail, and the smarter ones realized that it was easier, safer, and more lucrative to be at least nominally aboveboard. The punks had grown up. Now it was all money laundering and sweetheart land deals. But the essence of the system remained the same; every level was expected to pay for the protection it received from the one above, utility and loyalty were valued above everything else, everyone was compromised and vulnerable, and that way things ran smoothly.

"Why?"

"That's the question."

"You don't know the answer?"

"Not exactly."

"Has he done this before?"

"Not so drastically. We negotiate terms now and then—that's normal—but nothing like this."

"How much more is he asking?"

"Pretty much double what he asked before."

"And presumably the hike will play havoc with your margins."

"You could say that."

"He's doing this across the board with everyone who operates down here?"

"All the ones I know of, yes."

"So he needs money."

Bronson raised a sardonic eyebrow. "You're a genius."

"Why is he doing it?"

"Like I said, I don't know."

"But you have an inkling?"

Bronson was scared. Behind the shaved head and the beard and the iron slabs of muscle, he was scared, and that only meant one thing.

"Novak's leaning on you because he's being leaned on himself."

"You said that. Not me."

Novak was tight with the Kremlin and when someone was tight with the Kremlin, the only person who could lean on him was Putin himself. Everyone knew what happened to those who pushed back.

"What's he done wrong?" Arkady asked.

"You didn't hear this from me."

"Fine."

"And it may not even be true."

"But . . . ?"

"But it makes sense."

"Tell me."

"They say that Novak double-crossed him on the bridge deal."

"Which bridge?"

"The Kerch Bridge."

Novak would have gotten the contract because of his friendship with someone in the Kremlin. Infrastructure projects that big had to be signed off on by Putin personally, and of course he would expect a large cut of that himself. People amused and appalled themselves by trying to work out how much Putin was worth, and the figures went up to $275 billion and beyond. To Arkady, the question was moot. Putin was worth what the Russian state was worth, no more, no less.

"That bridge was a two-billion-dollar project."

"Exactly. Novak started withholding money as Putin was waiting for his cut. Imagine the kind of sums we're talking about," Bronson said.

Arkady could. The numbers were theoretical, but he knew what men would do for them.

★　★　★

Elena and Karina came out of the café. Backlit by the climbing sun, they reminded Arkady of one of the old Soviet propaganda posters representing happy, healthy citizens marching together arm in arm. It was the first time, Arkady reflected, that he had seen Elena smile, really smile, since they'd left Kyiv.

"Karina," he said, "can I drop you off at your office? I have something I want to ask you on the way."

"Sure, happy to." She got in the backseat.

He looked in the rearview mirror and, as expected, the FSB were right behind them.

"How much do you know about the Kerch Bridge deal?"

Karina's hand flew to her mouth. "How do *you* know about that?"

Whatever father and daughter talked about, Arkady thought, it was not this.

"That doesn't matter. Do you have enough to bring him down?"

"I have enough to set things in motion."

The fog was lifting, Arkady thought, but not enough. He could glimpse outlines where before there had been nothing. He needed more. He could ask Karina not to go public with what she knew about the bridge, and hope that in doing so he could buy enough time to find if and how this was connected to the murders, but he had no guarantee that it was. If, on the other hand, exposing Novak set in motion a chain of events which brought other things to light, that could work in Arkady's favor.

"How would you do that?"

"Leak it to the press," she said. "A story like this is manna to a proper investigative reporter, and even in this country there are still a few of those left."

"Well, if you need the name of one, I know Tatiana Petrovna."

Karina was smiling. "I've already asked her down."

Of course, Arkady thought. Karina had overseen media relations for Forum. Naturally, she'd have known Tatiana. And when Tatiana appeared on TV after Uzeir Osmanov's murder, Karina called and told her to get down to Crimea, because here was where the story was: the Crimean Tatars, the Werewolves coming to town, and something bigger than both of those combined, which Karina was working on and which she would hand over when she knew it would pass inspection. And the real genius of the story was that even if the public was too jaded to care about an obscenely rich man making himself even richer, it wasn't their reaction that was important. The Kremlin would never allow the humiliation of being so openly ripped off to pass unavenged. Putin himself would have to act against Novak. It was a small victory, but Leonid Lebedev had been right: even small victories were better than no victories.

"Karina's got us VIP tickets for 'Russian Reactor' tonight," Elena said.

"What's that?"

"Opening night of the Werewolves show. They do it every year," said Karina.

"What kind of show?"

"Motorbikes, historical reenactments, fireworks."

"Why would I want to go to that? Why do *you* want to go to that?"

"I have to go," Karina said. "Novak is guest of honor. I'd like to go with some friends. It should be entertaining. Besides, it's just down the road from you."

"Where?"

"They've been setting up in the old Inkerman quarry since they got here."

26

The show began at sunset. Thousands of people had arrived over the course of the evening; families, young men with shaved heads, gaggles of teenage girls, men in ill-fitting army surplus. There were bikers, too, either recreational or members of other clubs, and they moved carefully around the Werewolves, laughing nervously as they tried to hide their fear and awe. People had brought picnic food, beer, and vodka, and if they hadn't, there were stalls that sold kebabs, burgers, and alcohol. Everyone found their spot on the wide expanse of grass in front of the main stage and settled in for the evening. Some had even brought tents. Arkady saw that the Black Sea Fleet had set up a recruiting booth.

There had been an underground city here in the eighth century. Water from the Black River had carved hundreds of large and small caves into soft limestone. A Byzantine monastery was built in one of these caves. Many other structures followed, including a cave fortress for which Inkerman was named. The Russians quarried the beautiful white sandstone to restore Sevastopol after the Second World War. Now the quarry was closed, and the caves were used by the Inkerman winery to store barrels of wine. History was never buried, not even when it was underground.

The stage was vast, towering four stories above the ground. Even from the VIP area where Arkady and Elena were sitting in folding chairs, it felt intimidatingly large. There were ramps leading down to ground level, presumably for motorbikes to enter and leave. The edifice was flanked by a Yak-7 fighter plane on one side and a T-34 tank on the other, both vintage-era 1940s. Arkady couldn't tell from this distance whether they were the genuine article or replicas but, either way, he recognized them instantly, the legacy of a father who had been a general in the Red Army.

Elena shuddered. "It's as if nothing has moved on in all this time," she said.

"Yes."

"My father would be horrified if he knew I was here."

"It's important to know your enemy," Arkady said.

"I know them perfectly well," she said.

Novak and Yashin were walking across the open grounds together, and they could hardly go more than a few feet without being stopped for a word, a handshake, or a selfie. Arkady couldn't tell how much people wanted to see Yashin and how much they wanted to see Novak, but he guessed that the point was moot.

Tatiana walked behind Novak and Yashin, writing on a notepad, watching and listening as she always did. Karina was at her side, and Arkady understood how she would have spun this to get Tatiana access. This was the *New York Times*, and the whole world would read her story. He wondered whether Novak had any idea what would happen when her story was published.

They walked past a Werewolf's bike which had been left unattended. Yashin gestured toward it, indicating he wanted it moved. As far as Arkady could see, most of the Werewolves were now backstage or waiting in the wings. No one responded. Yashin gestured again. Novak turned to Karina and said something. She nodded, threw one leg across the saddle, fired the engine up, and began to weave slowly through the crowds.

It was a big motorcycle, Arkady saw, but she road it with ease.

One of the Werewolves pointed to something on the saddle behind her, a leather vest. Karina turned, took one hand off the bars while still riding, picked the vest up, and threw it over to the Werewolf. The bike hadn't even wobbled.

Arkady thought he must be mistaken.

He glanced at Elena. She was looking at the stage and hadn't seen any of this.

"I'll be right back," he said.

He got up, left the VIP area, found a spot beneath the seating platform where he was unlikely to be overheard, and called Victor. It was half past eight: Sevastopol and Moscow were in the same time zone.

The phone rang.

"Arkady?"

"Right. Are you in Petrovka?"

"Yes. I swapped shifts with Mostovoi."

"Listen, I need you to find passenger manifests for flights to and from Kyiv around the time Uzeir Osmanov was shot."

"To and from which airports?"

"Start with Minsk and Warsaw. If you can, also trace back from either of those to Domodedovo or Sheremetyevo in Moscow." He needed to know whether Karina had been in Moscow when Alex and Leonid Lebedev were killed.

"Who am I looking for?"

"Karina Abakova."

There was a long silence. Arkady sensed Victor's shock as clearly as if they'd been in the same room.

"Does that mean what I think it means?"

"Yes. I think so. I don't know."

"Arkady, what the hell have you got yourself into?"

The loudspeaker boomed above Arkady's head—"THE SHOW WILL BEGIN IN FIVE MINUTES"—and he pressed his hand to his ear.

"Listen, Victor. I'm at a big event and it's hard to hear you, so text me what you find, can you?"

"Sure. I'm on it."

Arkady ended the call and went back up to his seat. Karina was there now, sitting on the other side of Elena, with Novak a couple of rows ahead of them, right at the front.

"Everything okay?" Elena asked.

"Fine. Just Victor checking in. No news."

He tried not to look at Karina. It was possible that he'd gotten it all wrong, that she was just someone who happened to be able to ride a motorcycle well, and that Victor would text back that Karina had not been to Kyiv recently. But Arkady had seen what he had seen, a visual memory of Karina throwing the leather vest for the Werewolf to catch; her body position, her balance, the way she moved, had all been identical to the moped rider in Kyiv.

Now, even the set of her face looked different. Over the past few days, he had seen her look distressed, contrite, and happy, but now all he saw was the concentration of a calculating mind. She was watching the stage as it went dark in preparation for the show to begin. He should get Elena away from there, but he couldn't without alerting Karina. The fact that Karina didn't know that he knew was his only advantage.

The stage lights went dark. In the distance, the pink sunset over the bay was fading. Arkady saw burning torches and wheels of fire. A drumroll thundered. The crowd whistled and cheered.

A single spotlight tracked Yashin as he walked slowly across the stage. There were more cheers. He waited for them to die down before letting his deep voice roll over the crowd.

"My fellow Russians, welcome! Tonight, I invite you to join me on a journey through the history of our great country. Are you ready?"

"Yes!" they shouted.

"Louder. Are you ready?"

"Yes!"

More spotlights flicked on one by one, hunting like searchlights. Tsar Nicholas at a desk, signing his own abdication treaty. His wife and children. Bolshevik soldiers. The spotlights skittered around the stage, crisscrossed, merged, disentangled, as the Romanovs ran this way and that and the soldiers chased and corralled them. Finally, up against the wall, they pleaded for their lives. The Bolsheviks unleashed a barrage of bullets, so loud and realistic that some of the crowd near the stage winced.

It occurred to Arkady that this was a hugely expensive extravaganza, like the Olympics. Russia had to be paying for it.

Now came burning buildings as men in red battled men in white. "Hatred mixed with a dream," intoned Yashin over the loudspeakers, and Arkady realized with a start that Yashin was standing in a pulpit on a platform just beyond the VIP section. The crest of the Red Army had been painted on the pulpit, giving him the air of a ghost, half preacher, half general.

"Here were the gates to hell, where only the righteous survived."

Arkady held up his phone as though he wanted to film some of the performance. Nothing from Victor yet.

Stalin, an actor dressed all in white, climbed out of an old limousine. Smoke belched as men dressed in overalls mimed long hours working in factories. After them came the miners, faces blackened with soot. The sounds of machinery clanking and whining reverberated through the speakers. Now the spotlights went off one by one until only one man was left, pounding away with a jackhammer.

"Aleksey Grigoriyevich Stakhanov," said Yashin. "Order of Lenin twice. Order of the Red Banner of Labor. Hero of Socialist Labor. Mined 227 tons of coal in a single shift, fifteen times his quota."

The crowd cheered again. Only in Russia, Arkady thought, could a coal miner be treated like a rock star.

His phone vibrated. He held it at arm's length to read Victor's text.

DME—MSQ 17 Jun. MSQ—KBP 18 Jun. Working on returns.

Those were the airport codes. Domodedovo, Minsk, and Kyiv respectively. She had flown from Moscow's Domodedovo airport to Minsk in Belarus and then to Kyiv on June 18, 2021.

Uzeir had been killed on the nineteenth.

Arkady stole another glance at Karina. She looked like just another rapt spectator.

Two men sat at a table, signed a treaty, shook hands. Molotov and Ribbentrop. Ribbentrop grinned at the crowd as he left the stage, tearing up his copy and letting the paper fall from his hands. Arkady heard boos.

Hitler was speaking, his image projected onto the back wall of the stage. It was footage absorbed in the popular culture by osmosis, the staccato black and white, the jabbing hands, the rage and the lick of hair falling across his forehead. More boos, louder this time. An air raid siren wailed. Shadows of bombers flew across the roof of the stage. There were explosions and clouds of smoke. The Wehrmacht swept across the stage in Panzer tanks and SS soldiers forced men to kneel and shot them in the back of the head. They loaded the women and children onto flatbed trucks.

"The fascists thought it would be easy. They hadn't counted on the heroism of the Russians."

A man billowing flames appeared at a balcony and leapt, a mother clasped her baby to her chest and ran for cover. Young men scaled walls, threw grenades. Hand-to-hand fighting in

urban streets. Stalingrad, Moscow, Leningrad. Nurses came
out with knives and stabbed Nazis where they stood, snipers
lay in the eaves and scattered the enemy. A concert pianist in
black tie was rolled onto the stage. Arkady recognized the re-
frain. He was playing from the fourth and final movement of
Shostakovich's seventh symphony, originally titled "Victory."

"This was the war of good against evil, light against shadow,
love against hate, paradise against hell . . . until eventually,
broken, the humiliated Nazis retreated. The light of the Holy
Grail lit up the darkest years of Russian grief. The Russian
state prevailed and, in the end, triumphed."

Arkady's phone vibrated again.

KBP—MSQ—DME 20 Jun. DME—SIP 21 Jun.

He texted back.

Please check SIP—DME flights for days before Alex's murder.

Three dots while Victor replied.

On it.

The proletariat began to rebuild. Trampolinists flew and
twisted between giant hammers and anvils. Women in shorts
and vests leapt from the bikers' pillion seats onto the stage.
The hammer and sickle sat inside a red star on their chests.
They moved in rhythm to the marching music. Stalin himself
began to sing. Gagarin was going up into space with Strauss's
fanfare playing all around him in eruptions of brass and blaz-

ing organ. What else could you use but Stanley Kubrick's space theme from *2001*?

Alex's words came to Arkady. "HAL, the computer in *2001*—you know why he called it that? Because in English the letters *H*, *A*, and *L* come right before *I*, *B*, and *M*. IBM, see?"

It was all coming too fast. Too much noise around him, the rocket blasting off from a model Baikonur Cosmodrome while Yashin spoke of how the space race was all Soviet. He shook his head, forced himself to concentrate.

From HAL to IBM. Alex had sent Arkady pictures of Gogol, Tolstoy, and Chekhov the night before he was killed. In that order? Arkady was pretty sure, but he couldn't remember beyond all doubt. He began to flick back through the message folder.

Karina looked across at him and gestured to the show.

He smiled, pointed at his phone, and made a yapping gesture with his hand. She smiled and nodded.

He nodded back.

For some reason, he was the one who felt treacherous. He dragged his thoughts back to Alex's message. There it was. Gogol, Tolstoy, and Chekhov, in that order, just as he'd remembered. He wasn't totally losing his mind, then.

Another text from Victor.

SIP—DME 12 Jun.

He texted back. **Flight time please.**
Three dots again.

SIP 2055 DME 2315.

She could have arrived late at night, met Alex early the next morning, and killed him. If Alex had texted Arkady with what he'd found, maybe he'd texted Karina, too, perhaps asked her for an explanation. She hadn't responded to anybody else's texts, only Alex's.

Gogol, Tolstoy, Chekhov. IBM. HAL.

The answer was so obvious that Arkady cursed himself for not having seen it earlier.

His English was still good enough for him to remember that alphabet, even if it took him a moment or so. One letter back from *G* was *F*. One letter back from *T* was *S*. And one letter back from *C* was *B*.

FSB.

It didn't make sense. It all made perfect sense.

An actor playing Gorbachev appeared, and the malevolence hurled in his direction was so instant and extreme that Arkady felt himself recoil. Gorbachev signed away the union and got off stage quicker than he'd arrived, pursued by a very weary man in a bear costume. Oligarchs connived to divide the economy between themselves. Pro-Western demonstrators marched back and forth across the stage in perfect time with vast metal puppet hands, which waggled malevolently above them. Arkady noticed that one of the puppet hands sported a ring emblazoned with a logo similar to the American presidential seal. And now came the Werewolves themselves for the climax, riding in formation, Russian flags flying high off the backs of their bikes. Fire spat from their exhausts as they rode through silver rings, turned, and came through again. Percussionists banged oil drums in front of a waterfall dripping molten gold.

"Excuse me." Karina was trying to get past Arkady.

"You're leaving?"

"Have to sort stuff out for the after show," she said.

He moved aside to let her by and turned to Elena. "You okay?"

"Just about."

"I'll be right back." He squeezed her shoulder and hurried out of the VIP area and down the steps, scanning to see where Karina had gone.

There. She was walking toward the side of the stage. Arkady followed her. A Werewolf let her through and challenged him. He showed his badge and the Werewolf stepped aside. If the man thought he was down here on Kremlin orders, then Arkady wasn't in a hurry to disabuse him.

Karina was walking purposefully ten feet ahead. Arkady hung back, wanting to keep her in sight without being seen. He would have no plausible explanation as to why he was backstage.

The superstructure of the stage loomed high to their left. Karina opened a door and disappeared. Arkady followed her. The door was swinging back when he reached it, caught it, and quietly pushed it open. He stepped inside.

He was in the guts of the stage. Scaffolding climbed all around him in arteries and veins of steel. The light from the main stage had dimmed by the time it got to the outer reaches here, but there was still enough for Arkady to see where he was going. How was he ever going to climb scaffolding when he could barely climb a single flight of stairs without stumbling?

Karina's footsteps clanged above him. He caught a glimpse of her legs as she climbed a ladder, traversed a walkway, and climbed another ladder. Again he quietly followed.

"Sort stuff out for the after show," she had said. Drinks, canapés—that was the presumption. Strange place to keep them.

He had sight of her, lost her, caught sight of her again. Where was she going?

The music began to crescendo. Arkady felt it shake the ladder—or was he shaking the ladder? For a moment he thought that he might fall. He pulled himself up the last few rungs to the next planked walkway and crouched down, trying to regain his balance and stop the shaking. Light blazed in kaleidoscopes of color. The crowd roared, subsided, roared again. Louder, brighter, more intense, then suddenly everything went dark and silent.

He counted a beat, maybe two, before the applause began. Not the kind of polite applause one might find at a classical concert but something altogether more visceral and atavistic. The noise seemed to come from the depths of the soil itself. Here, even for a short time, the faithful had seen the Russia of their dreams, the Russia they worshipped and adored and believed in, the Russia which took on the world and won because it was the last, greatest beacon of hope. This was not the Russia of their everyday drabness, where a man in an office demanded your rubles to do his job, or where the apartment above flooded into yours because the owner had left the tap running while drinking himself into a stupor. This was Russia through the looking glass, a past long gone but a future which was still theirs to take, unbowed, unbent, unbroken.

The lights came back on. Arkady lifted a hand, screwed up his eyes, turned his head away, opened his eyes again, and looked for Karina.

She was gone.

He looked ahead to where he'd last seen her and to his left and right, but all he saw were empty walkways.

She couldn't have come back past him, he thought. Chances were that she'd just kept going. He set out in the same direction. The applause was still going on. He doubted that she'd be able to hear his footsteps over that. He quickened his pace.

The walkways were leading gradually around. He glanced down through a gap and saw that he was high above the middle of the stage. Yashin was bowing to the audience and pointing left and right as he acknowledged the other bikers and actors. Arkady saw Novak bounding up to share the moment.

Now Arkady knew.

He looked up. There was another walkway above him. He ran to the nearest ladder, no longer caring if she heard him.

Yashin's voice came loud over the speakers. "Rossia! Rossia!"

They took up the chant, deep and sonorous. "RO-SSI-YA! RO-SSI-YA!"

Arkady grabbed at the rungs. His hands were slick with sweat. He wiped them on his trousers and tried again. He was clumsier now. One foot slipped as he climbed, his shin hitting against the metal. He gritted his teeth and kept climbing.

Finally reaching the highest walkway, he saw her. She was on one knee, an AK-47 rifle resting on a horizontal metal bar. The backs of the stage lights were just in front of her, rendering her totally invisible to anyone out front. Novak and Yashin were straight ahead of her on a forty-five-degree angle, fifty feet away, no more. They had their backs to her.

"RO-SSI-YA! RO-SSI-YA! RO-SSI-YA!"

A gilded coat of arms was being winched up above the

stage. It bore a Soviet star, a tsarist double-headed eagle, and ears of wheat. The crowd watched, cheered, and chanted.

Arkady heard military fireworks: the whoosh of rockets, the dull boom of shells, the rat-tat-tat of gunfire. Colors exploded in the night sky.

Karina's eye was at the sight. She was perfectly still. This was when she would shoot: now, with all the noise and explosions around. It was the perfect cover, a way of ensuring no one would be able to even hear it, let alone tell where the shot had come from.

"Karina!" Arkady yelled. "Karina!"

She didn't hear. He had no weapon, nothing to distract her with. If he ran, he wouldn't get there in time. He was too far away. He ran anyway.

Her face was pure concentration. Noise, lights, and people moving, and amid all this she was the one still point.

Inhale. Exhale. Inhale. Exhale. Take the shot between breaths.

Inhale.

Hold.

Fire.

27

It was Novak. Novak with a constellation of red where his head used to be, and Yashin turning away in horror as he was sprayed with blood and tissue. Yashin couldn't have been in on the plot. No one who knew that Novak was going to be shot would stand that close to him.

The realization of what had happened rippled out in waves. First Yashin and the nearest Werewolves, then the actors on-stage, and finally the crowd, beginning at the front. Fireworks illuminated faces and painted their shock in Technicolor. People turned and tried to push their way through the crowd, coming up hard against those still working it out. It was a recipe for panic.

Karina turned and saw him. Her expression was neither surprised nor outraged, just blank. A split-second assessment and cold calculation and then she turned the rifle toward him and brought it up to her shoulder.

He threw himself at her more through instinct than anything else. The impact pushed the gun barrel up and away even as she fired. Arkady heard a roaring in his ears. Still holding her rifle, Karina tried to push Arkady off. He pressed his weight harder to hold her down, knowing that physical strength was the only advantage he had, and even that might not be enough. Parkinson's had seen to that.

She scratched at his face. He turned his head and her nails hit his cheek. She had been going for his eyes. FSB techniques, he thought, balls and eyes. Fight dirty, and if that doesn't work, fight dirtier.

Karina was still trying to get the rifle out from between them. Arkady grabbed one of her hands with his own to pry it open. She screamed, spat at him, tried to bite. He felt her grip loosen. The rifle came free. He had hold of it for a moment and was trying to get a better grip when she brought her knee up and knocked it away. It fell from his hands, bounced on the walkway, and began to tumble over the side toward the stage below. Karina grabbed for it. Arkady kicked out, smashing her hand against the railings, and from her cry he knew he had broken it. He watched as the gun landed on the stage, not far from where a couple of Werewolves were kneeling by Novak's prone figure. No one noticed.

Karina threw a punch with her other hand. Arkady got his own hand up in time to block and hold it.

"You have to come with me," he said.

He was still holding on to her hand. She twisted her body and kicked him as hard as she could in the side, sending the air rushing from his lungs. He wasn't aware of having let her go, but as he doubled over and tried to suck oxygen back in, he felt the shuddering of the walkway as she ran.

He pushed himself upright. The air came slowly back.

Karina was long gone. Arkady retraced his steps back down to ground level, pressing himself close to the ladders as he descended. His lack of balance was making him wobbly, and when he slipped on the last part of the descent and half fell the last few feet, he was only glad that it hadn't been worse.

No one saw him come out of the superstructure, and even if they had, he doubted that anyone would have cared. People were running, shouting, and crying. Arkady headed back toward Elena. Two Werewolves on bikes passed on either side of him and he hardly noticed them.

The VIP section was practically empty. There were only a handful of people there, and none of them were Elena. Arkady dialed her number but there was no signal. That figured. Crowds overloaded mobile networks all the time, and this was a crowd that, half-crazed with fear, was trying to call loved ones.

He jostled his way to the staircase leading up to the VIP section and climbed up the first flight, just to get a vantage point. How could he possibly hope to pick Elena out in the crowd, and even if he could, how would he catch her attention?

He scanned back and forth. There was no sign of her. The fireworks were still exploding overhead. They reminded Arkady of nighttime bombing raids, phosphorus illumination and tracer fire.

There was no point in staying here. He decided to head

back to the apartment, hoping that Elena would be there. He also had to report what Karina had done, and he needed to be smart about whom he told.

If Karina had told Yashin what she had done and who had seen her, then they'd be looking for him. They'd grab him before he got out of here, and after that all bets were off. Yashin would no longer be offering all the help he could while fulminating against the evils of pederasty and Satanism. Arkady was witness to a murder, and witnesses to murders like these tended to be discredited, eliminated, or both.

He hurried down the steps again and joined the exodus. The crowd moved forward, stopped, moved forward again. Men shouted in frustration and children cried.

Four Werewolves roared along the outside of the perimeter fence, their engines so loud that already nervous spectators flinched. Arkady saw them arc around a corner and take up positions by the main gates, two on each side. They made no attempt to get people through more quickly or to control the panic. They were simply scanning the people leaving, looking for someone.

Looking for him.

Arkady turned in a slow 360. He was hemmed in on all sides. Trying to go back and find another way out was impossible and in any case risked drawing attention to himself. It was this way or not at all.

They drew closer to the gates. The Werewolves kept looking, checking. Arkady took a step closer to the man in front and lowered his head slightly—not so much to be hidden as just enough to make him harder to recognize. He thought about bending down, pretending to tie a shoelace, but again that risked more than it might save. Remember the lessons of Soviet times, he thought. Follow the crowd, don't stand out, be the gray man.

Arkady was almost level with the Werewolves now. He tried to clear his mind of everything except the next few seconds and kept his eyes fixed on the man in front of him. The crowd slowed, almost stopped, kept moving. Arkady waited for the shout, the rough hand on the shoulder. It would almost be better for it to come that way, if only to end the torture of anticipation. He shuffled, stepped, shuffled.

The crowd around him began to disperse. They were past the gates. Arkady risked the briefest of glances back at the Werewolves. They were still watching the crowds, still looking for him.

He walked as quickly as he dared. Most people seemed to be heading back to their cars or to catch buses headed for Sevastopol. Relatively few had reason to stay in a quiet suburb like Inkerman. He tried Elena again and finally he got through.

"Arkady! Are you all right?"

"I'm fine. Are you?"

"Yes. Scared, though. Did you see—"

"How far are you from the apartment?" Arkady asked.

"Five minutes or so."

"I think we should stay away from there for now. Remember the wine bar around the corner from our apartment?"

"Yes."

"I'll meet you there."

"What's going on?"

"I'll tell you when I see you, but don't talk to anyone else."

★   ★   ★

His eyes had to adjust to the dim light before he could see Elena waving from a booth in the back. Hardly anyone was there, but a TV blared at the rear of the bar.

She had already ordered two glasses of wine. He sat across from her and, in a hushed tone, told her as quickly and concisely as he could what had happened up in the scaffolding.

"Karina?" Elena shook her head, tried again. "Karina?"

"She's been deceiving you—everyone—all along. She's FSB, and I'm sure she was sent in to infiltrate Forum."

It had to have been Karina who had cleverly planted the FSB watchers at every Forum rally. It was classic legerdemain: here's where they wanted you to look, while all the time a mole went about her business undisturbed and undetected.

"But why kill Novak?"

"Because he double-crossed Putin over the Kerch Bridge deal. This way, Putin not only gets rid of someone who is stealing from him, he also sends a message to anyone else thinking of going up against him."

"There has to be more to it than that."

Yes, Arkady thought, there did have to be. If Karina's murder of Alex had been a simple response to him having discovered her real identity, the same did not apply to Leonid Lebedev and Uzeir Osmanov. Those had been political assassinations, figures of influence targeted for what they had represented rather than what they had known or done.

His phone rang. It was Victor.

"Arkady, we just heard about Novak."

"It was Karina."

"What?"

"It's true. You're the first person I've told. It was Karina. I saw it with my own eyes, and if she could have killed me, too, she would have."

"Why?"

"She has been working for the FSB all along."

Victor whistled. "I've got someone who wants to talk to you," he said.

"Renko." Arkady knew even before Zurin spoke that it would be him. "How are your investigations going?"

"Satisfactory in some ways, less so in others."

"How so?"

"I've found the person responsible for the murders but I don't have her in custody, and even if I did, she has some powerful friends who would, I'm sure, set her free."

"Then we understand each other."

"In general or in this specific case?"

Zurin laughed. "Always the need for accuracy. That's why you're good at your job."

"That doesn't answer my question."

"Persistent too." Zurin cleared his throat. "What you saw, Renko, you only have your own eyewitness testimony, right?"

"And a scratch on my cheek which looks like a Siberian tiger attacked me."

"A scratch which, I'm sure, could have any number of explanations. A clumsy fall, a jealous lover."

"You can't wish this one away."

"Oh, but I can. And I do, and I will, and you will. It never

209

happened. And if you say it did, it will be dismissed as the rantings of a burned-out investigator with health problems. Don't end a distinguished career this way."

Arkady hung up. Obviously, the FSB had gotten to Zurin.

The bartender turned up the television. A breathless reporter was broadcasting live from the quarry, interviewing anyone she could get her hands on. Police lights whirled in the background.

"Governor Novak has been shot. We don't know his condition yet." Arkady knew that no one survived a head shot like that.

She spoke for a long time, finding new ways to tell her audience that she had no concrete information. There was a skill in that, Arkady conceded, and maybe it was a skill he should have learned earlier in his career.

The studio anchor was talking now.

"Ludmilla, let me stop you there. The authorities have just released a picture of the woman suspected of shooting Governor Novak."

Arkady felt a sudden surge of righteous anger toward Zurin. It never happened? No one would believe him? It was all over the airwaves!

"This is the suspect—we're just getting that picture up for you now. Police have advised members of the public to call them if they see her but not to approach her directly. Her name is Elena Osmanova." The picture was of her too.

And now, finally, the fog lifted and Arkady saw the plot in full.

What did Putin want? To eliminate all rivals who threatened his own power base, who tried to steal from him, or both. And eliminate any sense that Russian territory could be inhabited by anybody but Russians. It wasn't enough for Novak to be killed. He had to be killed by a member of the Tatar community, and not by just any Tartar but by one whose own father had been their leader and could therefore be portrayed as crazed with grief. And that in turn would allow Putin to order a crackdown on the Tatars while putting a more pliant man in the Governor's office.

This was straight out of the Kremlin playbook. One of Putin's first actions in power was rumored to have been just that: deliberate bombings of apartment blocks, which were then blamed on the Chechens and used as justification for reducing Grozny to rubble. Distort, deceive, divide, defeat.

Arkady wondered when the decision to frame Elena had been made. When they first turned up in Sevastopol? Or had it been more recent? He didn't know and it didn't matter. What mattered was that at some stage the decision had been made to frame Elena for it, and that was cynicism beyond even Arkady's comprehension.

News of the assassination had reached the streets. Customers came in and talked about nothing else. Drinks in hand, they clustered around the TV.

He called Tatiana. She answered instantly.

"Arkady! Tell me it's not true."

"Of course it's not true. Can you help us?"

"Anything."

"Will you come and get us?"

"Where are you?"

"In Inkerman, in a little bar called the Wine Bar on Mansur Mazinov Street. Number 240. Do you think you can find that?"

"No, but my phone will. I'm leaving now."

"We'll be in an alley right next to the bar."

He ended the call. Elena was looking at him.

"She must really care for you."

"She cares more about doing the right thing."

More customers arrived now looking for empty seats in the back. Arkady put money on the bar and they walked out arm and arm as any couple might on a Saturday night.

The alley was dark and offered at least some cover, but every time a car drove past, they shrank back against the wall. Arkady wondered how the FSB were doing back at their apartment. He had often been tempted to try to second-guess his quarry's movements, and as often as not he had tripped himself up by trying to be too clever. His strategy was simple now; he could only worry about getting Elena safely out of sight.

"What car is Tatiana driving?" Elena asked.

"I forgot to ask."

Eventually a car came down the road at the kind of pace which suggested the driver was looking for someone or something. Arkady peered out, saw that the driver was alone, and stepped out raising his hand. The car pulled over and the window came down. Tatiana smiled at him.

Arkady gestured for Elena to come. They piled into the back together.

"Do I get a chauffeur's cap too?" Tatiana asked. "Turn your phones off now, by the way. You don't want to be tracked by them."

She drove carefully among the little twisty streets until she got to the main road.

"We're passing our apartment. Drive a little slower?" Arkady asked.

A man with a rifle was standing next to Arkady's parked car and looking up at the lights in their apartment. Shadows moved behind their curtains. The main door to the building was smashed half off its hinges. Definitely FSB. He wondered whether the damage would come out of his deposit.

"Thanks."

"Lucky you didn't go back. I have a spare room in my apartment you'll be safe in."

"You're not in a hotel?"

"Airbnb."

"On a *New York Times* bank account?"

"Nobody's reading newspapers anymore. They had to cut back."

The Airbnb she was staying in was just to the north of the city center. They passed five police cars that for once weren't just scraping up late-night drunks. Arkady recognized that a lot of it was theater policing, cars racing down streets with flashing blue lights to reassure the citizenry. A major public figure had been killed, and they needed to at least seem to be doing something about it.

Elena crouched, keeping her head below the window. "There's a bottle of vodka on the floor," Tatiana said.

"Plus half a dozen more in the trunk," Arkady replied.

Tatiana smiled. She never went on any story without arming herself with copious quantities of vodka. Nothing else was such an all-purpose tool for a journalist; a bribe to gain access, a drink to loosen reluctant tongues, and a way to say thanks.

Arkady found the bottle, unscrewed the top, and handed it to Elena.

"I never felt less like getting drunk," she said.

Arkady tipped the bottle back and drank more than just a mouthful.

They arrived at Tatiana's five-story apartment building. She let the engine idle a moment after parking, checking up and down the street to see whether anyone was watching, then led them from the car, in through the door, and up to her apartment.

"Maybe I should just give myself up," Elena said.

"You're going to do no such thing," Tatiana replied.

Here was Arkady's former lover treating his current one like an errant child, and it seemed no less normal than anything else.

"I'm a danger to both you and Arkady," Elena said.

Arkady and Tatiana glanced at each other. Neither of them wanted to appear like parents giving Elena a lesson on how the world worked.

"They're framing you for a good reason," Arkady said. "They know you didn't do it. But to admit that would mean they'd have to reveal who did, and they're not going to do that."

"Besides," Tatiana added, "Arkady is already in as much danger as you are. More, maybe. He's the only witness to the shooting. They might want to imprison and try you, but they want to kill him."

"So what do you suggest?" Elena said.

"We have to get out of here," Arkady replied.

"Here as in where? This apartment? Sevastopol? Crimea?"

"The last. We have to get back into Ukraine."

"That's insane," Elena said.

"How about this?" Tatiana suggested. "We could go for the border right now, the three of us. It's three hours' drive, give or take. Kalanchak or Chonhar, take your pick; they're pretty much equidistant from here."

Arkady remembered Tatiana when she was in this mood, throwing up ideas and shooting them down like clay pigeons.

"We'd be too easily spotted," Arkady said. "Fewer cars at night, police checkpoints. Besides, those border posts probably aren't open twenty-four hours a day, so we'd have to wait for them to open."

"Plus they will have circulated your names to those posts," said Tatiana.

"Exactly."

"So while it's tempting just to go now, it risks more than it's worth."

"Then what?" Elena asked.

"You stay here," Tatiana said. "Stay here for the rest of the night and tomorrow as well. There's food, there's drink, and no one knows you're here. Don't go out, whatever you do. I have to work tomorrow. I've already filed a piece on Novak's shooting, and, God knows, there will be more on it. But leave it to me. I'll think of something."

"You'll think of something?" Elena's voice was thick with sarcasm.

Arkady feared briefly that Tatiana would bite back—everyone was on edge, and he wouldn't have blamed her if she did—but instead she nodded calmly.

"Yes, I'll think of something. It's what I'm good at. Now, why don't you two try to get some sleep?"

"Probably not going to be as easy as all that." Elena's tone was softer.

"Of course not. But that's what I've learned from war zones. Sleep when you can."

★ ★ ★

Arkady lay awake in the dark. He wasn't conscious of sleeping, but each time he looked at his watch, another hour or so had gone by, so he figured he must have drifted off at some stage.

Elena stirred next to him. When he reached across to calm her, she didn't wake up. Tatiana was in her own room across the corridor. He wondered if she ever thought about him.

She had gone from his life and soon she'd be gone again, and still so much lay unresolved and unsaid between them. They had broached it at their first meeting in Nakhimov Square, and it had been he who had shut it down.

28

Tatiana was gone when Arkady woke up. He walked into the kitchen and found that she had left salami, cheese, pastries, and coffee in a thermos.

He switched on the TV and found the local news. Novak's assassination was still the lead story, and the news anchor was reporting within fifty feet of angry crowds protesting the death of their governor.

"The president is said to be considering imposing martial law," he said.

Arkady saw Crimean Tatars being taken away for questioning. The news framed it as rounding up those who were known to have been associated with Uzeir Osmanov. In the background of one shot, Arkady saw a large X spray-painted on adjacent doors and the sight made him shiver. In Nazi Germany, an X on Jewish homes indicated that the people who lived within were suspect and could at any time be taken away or shot. Now it was the Russians and pro-Russian Crimeans persecuting the Tartars in the same way.

This was how pogroms started, by marking out an enemy and ushering in violence. Stones hurled at windows, shattering glass, leaving shards in their frames like jagged guillotines. Doors that had been locked and barricaded would be broken down. The rioters would surge like ocean waves as they came barreling in, grabbing whatever they could hold. Then there were those who stood by impassively, in uniform and out. They folded their arms and nodded permission. It had happened before, in Russia and elsewhere. It could happen again, Arkady thought.

Elena came in, fiddling with her phone. Arkady saw the Apple logo on her home screen, grabbed it from her, and pressed POWER OFF until the screen went black again.

"What are you doing?" she asked.

He put the phone down on the table. "We shouldn't use our phones. They can track us with them."

"I was trying to find out what's going on. There will be people in the community who need to know that it's all a lie."

"They know already!"

Her face crumpled. It wasn't that she had been deliberately careless. She was under the kind of strain which breaks people, not all at once but little by little, like a sailor in the doldrums. She had lost everything—her father, her party leader, the person she thought was her best friend—and, worst of all, she was being framed for murder.

The day passed in fits and starts. Tatiana had drawn the blinds, and though Arkady didn't want to open them, he did sneak a peek from the corner once or twice, just to be sure that the FSB hadn't set up camp outside. He watched TV, tried to read a couple of books he found on the shelves, busied himself with putting together lunch. He wanted to be on the phone with Victor to hear how the men at Petrovka were reacting to Novak's death. Instead, he was trapped in this little apartment.

Elena cleaned the place from top to bottom. Anything that distracted her was good as far as Arkady was concerned.

"Would you like a hand?" he asked.

She laughed. "Generations of Soviet men have just turned over in their graves."

There was the old joke about International Women's Day when for one day a year Russian men did all the cooking and cleaning. They made such a hash of it that their women didn't ask them to do it for another 364 days. Most men made a mess of the housework deliberately, but Arkady had known a few who really tried to make the day as nice as possible for their spouses. They were the ones who always came in to work the next day looking like survivors from the Battle of Kursk.

Tatiana returned late in the afternoon. She had a photographer with her.

"This is Gennady. Don't worry, I've worked with him for years and would trust him with my life. Often have, in fact."

Arkady shook hands. Gennady couldn't have been much younger than he was, and in his face Arkady saw an adventurer. Men like Gennady were happy as long as they had their cameras and places to go. Arkady liked to travel, but he wasn't a nomad.

"So," Tatiana continued, "I told you I'd come up with a

plan, and I have. A few years ago I came down here to do a story about fishing in the Black Sea after the annexation. Fishermen were overfishing stocks in territorial waters and there were Ukrainian demands for compensation. One of the guys I interviewed was a captain on a trawler. I rang him today. He's about to set off for a week's trip, but he'll meet you offshore tonight."

"How will we get there?"

"Gennady's hired an outboard from the marina for twenty-four hours. He'll take you out there."

"Told them I wanted to get some pictures of the city from out to sea," Gennady said. "Not that they gave a fuck."

"The trawler is due to dock at Odessa in two days' time with its catch. They'll put you ashore there, or somewhere close by. If you're caught, you can't give him away. I had my work cut out persuading him as it is."

"How much?" Arkady asked Tatiana.

"How much what?"

"How much did you pay him?"

"Who says I paid him?"

"Even someone of your charm can't convince a man to take a risk like that for free."

"It doesn't matter."

"It does."

"Arkady, just take it as—" She glanced at Elena and stopped. Arkady wondered what she'd been about to say. As a friendly gesture? As a token of her love? As an apology for walking out? "Well, it doesn't matter what you take it as, as long as you take it."

"Thank you. I owe you."

"*We* owe you," Elena said.

"Yes," Tatiana said. "You do."

There was a knock at the door, sudden and loud. Tatiana looked at Arkady and raised her eyebrows. Arkady shook his head. Tatiana gestured to the bedroom where Arkady and Elena had slept. They hurried in. There was a key in the lock, privacy for anyone who wanted it, or the room could be locked off for other Airbnb guests. Tatiana shut the door behind them, locked it, and pocketed the key.

Arkady heard her go over to the front door and open it.

"Karina," Arkady heard Tatiana say. "Yes, of course. Come in, please."

29

It was like listening to the radio, trying to discern what was going on just from their voices.

"I'm sorry to barge in like this, but the *New York Times* were kind enough to give me your address."

"What a terrible shock this must be for you."

"It is."

"Let me introduce you to my friend, Robert. He was just about to leave."

Gennady shook Karina's hand. "Glad to meet you and sorry I can't stay." He gave Tatiana a quick kiss and left.

"Can I offer you something?"

"Thank you, no. Who was that?" said Karina.

"A good friend I work with sometimes. He's a photographer. Would you like me to write something about Novak and the man he was? A more personal piece than the strictly political one. I'd be delighted to do it of course."

"Maybe in a day or two. No, I'm here to ask if you've heard from Arkady."

"I saw him at the square the day the Werewolves arrived."

"And since then?"

"No."

"Not at all?"

"Not at all. We didn't end on especially good terms and I think he took it hard."

There was a pause. If the FSB had tracked his and Tatiana's phones last night, they would have been here long before now. Karina had to be acting on her own.

"You know he's with Elena, don't you?"

"I didn't ask about his private life," Tatiana said.

"For obvious reasons, we need to find her."

"'We'?"

"The police. We need to find her for what she's done but also for the sake of the Tatars. There are mobs out there destroying Tatar properties."

"I know. I've been covering it."

"We want to put an end to that. If Elena gives herself up, the rioting will stop."

"How would that work?"

"If I hear from Arkady, I can let you know."

"Thank you," said Tatiana.

A chair scraped as Karina got up. "This is a nice place you have here."

"Thanks. It's an Airbnb the *Times* is renting for me."

"Mind if I look around? A friend's coming over from Warsaw and I said I'd find her somewhere to stay."

"Be my guest."

224

Karina was too smart to go straight for the locked door. That would have given her true intentions away. She took her time, cooing over the color scheme in the kitchen and the bidet in the bathroom before coming back toward the bedrooms.

She looked in Tatiana's first. "Nice view. You must get the sun in the morning."

"I do. It wakes me up. I hate it."

Karina laughed.

And now Arkady heard her footsteps come closer. He watched the door handle. It rattled, stopped, rattled again. "What's in here?"

"Connecting door to the next apartment."

"Do you have a key?"

"No. Why?"

"They didn't give you a key?"

"Well, no. Deliberately not. I don't want people from next door coming in here, and I'm sure they don't want me going in there."

"True." Karina stepped away from the door. "You can imagine I have a thousand things to do, but thank you for your time."

"My pleasure."

"Oh—why are all the blinds closed? Nice sunny afternoon like this, I'd want all the light I could get."

"It's difficult for me to write on my computer when it's so bright. Too much reflection."

Two sets of footsteps, the sound of a door opening and closing again, and then one set of footsteps approaching. Tatiana unlocked the door.

"I can't believe it," Elena said. "She came to kill Arkady!"

225

"If she had found me, she would have killed all three of us," Arkady said.

"Was she alone?"

"Yes."

"Surprising. I guess she doesn't want the FSB to know that she didn't eliminate me once she realized I had witnessed all of it. They would see it as a serious failure on her part. The *Times* should never have let her know your address."

"They knew that she was one of my contacts in Moscow, so they weren't suspicious, and obviously she told them a good story."

30

Gennady came back to the apartment and they waited until eleven before leaving. The trawler would be waiting two miles offshore at midnight, so this would give them just enough time to get there without taking the chance of being noticed.

Gennady went to get the car and spent five minutes outside, checking that no one was watching before sending Tatiana a text.

Got the pictures.

It was a basic subterfuge, but if the FSB had decided to monitor Tatiana's phone, it could be easily explained.

"Go," said Tatiana, hurrying them out the door.

Gennady drove. Arkady sat up front, and again Elena crouched down below the window line. Arkady checked in his side mirror for any car following them. Headlights flared, bobbed, menaced.

There was one car which seemed to be too persistent for comfort, always two or three car lengths back, spurning obvious chances to overtake other cars.

"Have we got time for a two-minute detour?" Arkady said.

"Two minutes, no more."

"Okay. Turn left here." He indicated a side street up ahead.

"You think we're being followed?" Gennady asked.

"I'm not sure."

Gennady turned left. Arkady kept his eyes glued to the mirror. Ten seconds later a pair of headlights turned off the road they had been on and began to follow them. The same car? A different one? Arkady couldn't tell.

Gennady was looking in the rearview mirror. "Left again?" he asked.

Arkady smiled despite himself. "You've been followed before."

"The best news photographers are always followed."

He swung the car left again.

Another ten seconds, and then the other car turned the corner and continued to follow them. Arkady looked in the side mirror.

There was a cross street up ahead. Turning left would take them back to the main road where they'd started. Three left turns was standard protocol for checking a tail. Turning right would lead them in another direction.

"Left?" Gennady asked.

"Please."

The turn signal ticked softly.

Gennady swung the car left a third time. Arkady didn't dare take his eyes off the mirror. If the following car also turned left, then what were they going to do?

The car behind them came to the junction. Arkady waited for the headlights as it turned left too.

The car instead paused and headed away from them. Next to him, Gennady wiped the back of his hand across his brow.

"Probably a drunk driver," Gennady said.

"You should have one of those stickers on your bumper: DON'T FOLLOW ME, I'M LOST, that kind of thing."

Gennady turned back onto the main road. Arkady tried to relax.

It was another ten minutes or so before the marina appeared on their right. Moonlight flickered across the water, and when they parked, Arkady heard the gentle wind chimes of rigging clanking against masts. Gennady got out, checked both ways, and beckoned for Arkady and Elena to get out. They slung their bags over their shoulders. Arkady noticed that Gennady had a camera bag.

"You're bringing that?"

"Of course. If I get stopped on the way back, I have to be able to tell them that I've been taking pictures of the city at night. Artistic shots from the water."

"And if we get stopped on the way out when Elena and I are still with you?"

"I'll say the same thing."

They walked down a pontoon pier with boats moored either side. Every other streetlight was out. Gennady peered through the gloom.

"There," he whispered.

It was a standard motorboat capable of seating six, eight at the most. No roof, no individual seats. Just benches.

Gennady sat in the stern, with Arkady amidships and Elena low in the bow. Gennady gripped the pull cord on the outboard motor and yanked. Nothing. He pulled again.

"It was working this afternoon," he whispered.

"Talk to it," Arkady said.

"Excuse me?"

"Pull cords are temperamental. Whisper undying love to it and it will start like a dream." Gennady was looking at him as though he'd lost his mind. "Go on."

Gennady shook his head, bent to the outboard, and whispered softly. He straightened up again and pulled the cord. The engine fired into life. In the quiet of the night, it sounded like a volcano erupting. Gennady adjusted the choke and let it settle to as low an idle as possible.

"Told you," Arkady said.

"You don't know what I said to it."

Gennady slipped the mooring ropes and twisted the throttle. The boat began to nose through the water. Arkady looked at his watch: 11:35.

"Plenty of time," Gennady said.

They crept clear of the marina. The wake glowed slightly as it churned in thin trails of phosphorescence behind them. Arkady let one hand trail in the water, needing to feel coolness on his skin. On a sunny day they would have been tourists out for a trip along the coast. Twelve hours' difference had made them fugitives.

Gray shapes loomed against the night sky. Arkady recognized them as some of the Black Sea Fleet warships. He looked for lights on board and saw none. Perhaps the sailors had traded the generator diesel for vodka. Perhaps they'd simply drunk the diesel instead. He remembered a story of a MiG fighter plane which had dropped out of the sky because the mechanics had drunk the antifreeze and replaced it with water. Victor had told him that story, had sworn it was true, and had laughed when Arkady had asked for proof. The point was, of course, not whether the story was true or not. The point was that it was plausible.

Would the fleet have patrol boats at night? If so, how often did they come around?

There was a bump against the boat, hard enough to knock Arkady off-balance.

"Fuck," Gennady said. "I must have hit something."

They were midway across the channel, in what was presumably the deepest part, so it was unlikely that they'd run aground. It had probably been a piece of debris. God knows what had ended up in this water. If you were dedicated enough, you could probably furnish a house sooner or later with what was floating here.

Arkady looked either side of the boat to see whether the debris floated past. A half-submerged oil drum, for example, could do some serious damage. He could see nothing.

Another bump, harder than the first.

"What was that?" said Elena from the bow.

Arkady turned and moved forward to see what she was looking at. The boat tipped slightly downward with his weight. He followed Elena's gaze and found himself looking into the unblinking eyes of a dolphin.

At another time he might have laughed.

Gennady pushed the tiller away from him and tried to steer around the dolphin. The dolphin went with them and bumped them for a third time, this one still harder. Up ahead, Arkady saw two more dorsal fins scything cleanly through the water toward them. Reinforcements.

The first dolphin clicked happily to his mates.

Gennady tried the other way. The dolphins battered against the boat as though hammering on drumskins.

"This is ridiculous," Gennady said, and gunned the engine. Arkady grabbed his hand and twisted the throttle back to idle.

"Arkady, what are you doing?" Elena said.

"We won't get through," Arkady replied.

"They're just *dolphins*," Gennady said.

"No, they're not 'just' dolphins. They're military-trained dolphins, and I saw them in action the other day. They belong to the Russian Black Sea Fleet. They won't let us through."

"Of course they'll let us through."

"No, they won't. We won't outrun them or dodge them. And if we try, we'll make so much noise that sooner or later the entire Black Sea Fleet will be awake, and then we really will be in danger."

"This is ridiculous." Gennady hawked a glob of sputum over the side. "Here's one I'll never live down at the Frontline Club. All those asshole war correspondents bragging about how they defused a land mine in Abkhazia with their bare

232

hands, and I have to be the guy who got turned back by dolphins. Dolphins!"

"Blame me and say they were orcas."

"Blame you? As in you really want me to turn around and go back?"

"Yes. I really want you to turn around and go back."

"Arkady!" Even at a whisper, Elena's voice was desperate. "You can't be serious!"

"There's no other way."

The dolphins were clustered around the bow and there were a couple on each side of the boat.

Elena looked at their military-like formation. The defiance went out of her. "I guess. But now what?"

"We'll have to find another way."

"It wouldn't be so bad if they weren't smiling at us," Gennady said.

"They're deadly serious."

Gennady backed the boat up a little and made a 180-degree turn.

The dolphins turned pirouettes as they went by.

31

Tatiana didn't waste time sympathizing. They had tried to escape, Arkady had decided that it was too dangerous, they had to come back. Even if they had wanted to try again, the dolphins would still be there and the trawler would be long gone.

"You can't stay here indefinitely," Tatiana said. "They will still be looking for you, and sooner or later they'll come back again."

"And if I have to stay here one more day," Elena said, "I'm going to lose my mind." She glanced at Tatiana. "No offense."

"None taken. So let's think. The only feasible way out is by road. You'll be picked up as soon as you set foot in an airport. By road, with Elena hidden somehow."

"We can't use my car," Arkady said.

"No. Even if the FSB haven't taken it away, they'll have put a tracker on it in case you come back and try to use it."

"The tracker will probably double its value."

She laughed. "At least."

"You could take my car," Gennady said.

"No, we can't do that."

"Why not?"

"It's a rental car."

"They have an office in Kyiv. Drop it off there."

"How will you get around?"

"Tatiana's car."

"And when I get to the border and my passport flashes every color of the rainbow on their computers?"

"Take this." Gennady held out his passport.

"No."

"Yes," Tatiana said. "You look passably like each other. They won't be looking for that car or that passport."

Arkady turned to Gennady. "What will you do without it?"

"I still have my ID card. I'll report the passport stolen when I get back to Moscow."

"If I get caught, you know how much trouble you'll be in?" Arkady asked.

"If you get caught," Tatiana replied, "you can say you stole the car and passport."

They would leave at dawn, figuring as before that it was safer to go during the day when there were more cars on the road and they were less likely to attract attention. Elena had curled up in bed and was sleeping. Gennady was doing the same on the sofa. Elena had said little since Arkady and Tatiana had formulated the plan, either figuring that this was the only possible way out or by now so exhausted that she was becoming resigned to whatever fate had in store for her. If they couldn't stay, they had to go. It wasn't much of a choice.

Arkady accepted that he wasn't going to sleep at all and went into the kitchen. He liked the quiet. Sometimes even everyday noise seemed too much, and alone with his thoughts was the only comfortable place to be.

Tatiana came and sat on the floor at Arkady's feet.

"Rub my shoulders, would you?"

He knew that this was not a come-on. She would never make a play for him while Elena was in the next room. No, it was not sex she wanted. It was something less, but also something more.

He placed his coffee cup on the table and rested his hands on her shoulders for a moment. Then he slid his hands down her back with his fingers pressing the muscles on either side of her spine. He knew her contours so well, he didn't have to look at what he was doing. Finally, at her hips, he slipped his hands under her blouse to feel her skin. She leaned back against his legs. A cat would have purred.

"Arkady, we can't," she said.

"Yes, I know." He brought his hands back up to her shoulders.

"Tell me something. There's something wrong, isn't there?"

"Wrong with what?"

"You."

He should have known that she of all people would notice.

"Yes. I have Parkinson's disease. What gave it away?"

She reached back and laid her hand on his. "I'm so sorry, Arkady. I guess it was the sort of hesitant way you're walking. What does Dr. Pavlova say?"

"She says the first thing that will go is my balance and maybe I'll have some shaking. I'll be able to live my life for years before it becomes really debilitating."

"How many years?"

"It's different with everyone, but I don't expect to see anything dramatic for at least five years."

"Well, I hope you know that, unless you marry Miss Osmanova, I will always be there to take care of you."

"Marry Elena?"

"Why not?"

"I'm not in love with her, for one thing."

Tatiana sighed. "I'm relieved."

"What will you do when we leave?"

"I'll write my piece for the *Times* identifying Karina Abakova as Novak's killer."

"Do you think they'll run it?"

"Yes. They're still getting news out. And the internet will publish it."

"Will you mention that she was probably the one who killed Leonid, Alex, and Uzeir?"

"I don't know that as a fact yet, but I might bring it up as a question to be investigated. I have to talk to the police too."

"What do you think will happen to her?"

"She'll be hard to find. She's probably already back in Russia. God knows what the Kremlin will do with her."

Arkady would have to break the news to Bronson. He would never understand how his daughter could have ended up working for the state.

"And where do you think you'll go?" Arkady asked.

"I still think Putin will invade Ukraine and I want to be there for that. I'll go to Kyiv. How about you?"

"I don't know."

How could he go back to Moscow? How could he continue to work for a man who refused to investigate murders that might reflect badly on the Kremlin? On the other hand, there was Zhenya and there was Victor.

"Will you try to be careful?" she asked. "And call me now and then?"

"Yes."

Neither of them wanted the night to end. They sat silently until dawn elbowed its way through the trees and pink clouds floated across the sky.

32

Arkady was Gennady, at least until they were safely across the border. He had memorized Gennady's date and place of birth. Did they look enough like each other to fool a passport check? Who knew? Arkady felt he looked nothing like his own passport picture, so perhaps he would look more like someone else's.

Elena lay on the backseat. She'd go in the trunk for the last stretch when they crossed the border, but she wasn't going to stay in the trunk for hours on end. Arkady considered arguing, but one look at Elena's face and he knew it wasn't worth it. They were both operating on thin margins as it was.

He eased the car away from the curb.

Traffic was light so early in the day, and they made good progress. It was no more than an hour until they were on the ring road around Simferopol. Smokestacks and factories lay to their right, apartment blocks on the left. The sun blazed above them. They spoke only once in that first hour when Arkady remarked on the whimsical nature of a sign to a village named Quince. Elena corrected him. It was a legacy from the Sürgünlik, she explained. When the Crimean Tatars had all been deported east, their villages were left empty and the order came down that they were to be renamed to help erase the memory of those who had lived there. A Simferopol newspaper was tasked with giving those villages new, Russian names. There were only two reference books in the newspaper office, one on growing fruit, the other on military history. That was why there was a village named Quince, and why there were other villages with names like Apricot, Tanks, and Guards.

Arkady laughed.

The road split just north of Simferopol. Going left would take them back along the route they had come in on, staying on the western side of the peninsula and crossing the border back into Ukraine at Kalanchak. Going right would take them on a northeast bearing to the Chonhar checkpoint. As Tatiana had said, the distances were pretty much equidistant.

On the way down, they had come through Kalanchak as Arkady Renko and Elena Osmanova, a couple together in Arkady's car. Now he would be trying to get back into Ukraine as a single man, Gennady, in a different car. The chances of an official at Kalanchak recognizing Arkady from before and noticing the discrepancies were small, perhaps even negligible, but they were not zero. All other things being equal, it made more sense to head to Chonhar.

He took the right-hand fork onto the M18. The fuel gauge flashed yellow at him. A sign by the side of the highway announced a gas station at Poltavka in ten kilometers.

"We're going to need to fill up," he said.

"Do you want me to get in the trunk?"

"No. Lie on the floor and pull the blanket over you."

"Okay."

She rolled off the backseat and onto the floor, arranging the blanket to cover herself. Arkady reached back and pushed their bags onto her.

"Comfortable?" he asked.

"It's practically the Ritz." Her voice was muffled through the wool.

"I'll be quick."

He rolled into the gas station, pulled up beside fuel pump number 4 and saw that the car filling up at pump number 5 belonged to traffic police.

He got out of the car, screwed open the gas cap, unhooked the nozzle, and began to fill the tank. The traffic cop, who seemed to be alone, glanced at him. An incurious glance, that's all it was, a normal part of everyday life. Arkady was a man filling his car at a highway service station. What could be less remarkable than that?

He had wild visions of the cop peering closer, radioing in a description, demanding his papers and handcuffing him. He felt his leg begin to tremble and he tensed it as subtly as he could against the ground to stop it. Parkinson's tended to act up at times like this.

The nozzle clicked off. He replaced it and began to head over to the station to pay. The cop was just ahead of him.

"You don't lock your car when you go inside?" said the cop.

"I'm only going in to pay."

"Takes a thief less time than that."

"I guess," said Arkady.

"You're too trusting."

"So they tell me."

There was a coffee machine in the corner. Arkady would have liked a cup of coffee, but he wanted to be in and out of here as fast as possible. The cop headed toward the machine. Arkady picked up a bag of barbecue potato chips, a cheese roll, and two bottles of water, then paid.

"All gassed up," Arkady said as he got back in the car. "Just driving out of the gas station now, so in a minute we'll be back on the highway and you can get up from there. I have some water and a cheese roll for you here."

"Thank God for that."

★ ★ ★

The road unwound ahead of him, and signs flashed names: KRASNYI PARTIZAN, NEKRASOVE, NOVOESTONIYA. Arkady concentrated on driving, nothing else. He would have liked to share the driving with Elena, but that was too dangerous. She had to remain hidden in the backseat. He would drive at least until they got to Ukraine. Then they could swap, but not before.

They spoke sporadically, no more. If anyone had glanced across and seen Arkady's mouth moving with no one else visible, what would they have thought? That he was on a hands-free call, perhaps, or that he was learning a new language from a tape. Maybe he was the kind of lunatic who spoke to himself on long car journeys.

They were just approaching Znam'yanka, about two-thirds

of the way to the border, when the car in front him had a blow-out. It happened both very fast and in slow motion. A Volvo station wagon was spinning and lurching as the wheel shed rubber in great chunks. He slammed on the brakes as the car ahead spun 180 degrees to face him. The driver's expression was one of sheer terror. Then the car kept on spinning, through a safety barrier and off the road, where it stopped in the grass.

Arkady pulled over without looking. A horn blared as the car behind swerved to avoid him. He stopped on the hard shoulder and put on his hazard lights.

"What are you doing?" Elena said.

"Going to see if she's okay."

"If who's okay?"

Elena wouldn't have seen the crash, of course.

"The woman ahead of us whose tire just blew."

"Arkady. We have to get to the border!"

"She could be badly hurt," Arkady said.

"Someone else will stop."

No, Arkady thought. You could never count on that.

"Get down on the floor as before. Blanket and bags."

"You're insane."

"Please, just do it."

"Take the keys with you, at least. I don't want someone stealing the car and driving off with me."

He turned off the engine, pocketed the keys, and got out. Arkady saw a truck approaching and stepped back.

He remembered, as he hurried toward the car, that plenty of accidents occurred when vehicles hit those parked on the hard shoulder. The first advice anyone was given when forced to pull over was to get out of the car. He couldn't risk that with

Elena. Perhaps she was right. Perhaps he should just get back in the car and let someone else deal with it. He couldn't.

The car was badly damaged. The hood had crumpled like cardboard in a compactor, the engine block visible and one wheel sticking out below at an angle. Protecting the driver was what the hood was supposed to do, Arkady knew, and if it looked bad, then it was still better than the alternative.

The driver was slumped against the wheel. Blood ran down the side of her face. It was hard to tell how old she was or even what she looked like. Her hair was light brown and he saw makeup on the parts of her face where the blood had not yet run. She looked at him with an open eye that did not move.

Arkady had seen enough dead bodies to know that this was one of them. He could tell from ten paces who was unconscious and who was dead, and it was nothing to do with seeing the rise and fall of a chest. It was something he could feel but not see, know but not articulate. He was not a religious man, and he set little credence by a soul or the supposed weight of one; twenty-one grams, supposedly. But standing here, on a warm morning by the side of a motorway, he felt the woman pass through him and go around him as her presence became an absence.

He checked her pulse anyway and held his fingers under her nose. Then he walked back to his own car, climbed inside, and closed the door.

33

They were fifteen miles from the border. Arkady drove until he found a secluded spot and an abandoned little dirt road that led down to fields and the sea beyond. He drove until they were out of sight of the highway. There were no houses overlooking them, only inlets and bays.

"Let's take a break," he said.

Elena peeled herself off the backseat and stumbled out of the car. She was shaking and Arkady held her until she calmed down.

"The border is ten minutes up ahead."

She stood looking out at the tranquil water, then began to pick her way through the tall grasses until she reached the water. Arkady followed.

"I'd like to stay here forever."

"Yes," he said.

They sat on the rocky beach leaning against each other and

gazed out to sea. A slight breeze played in her hair and every so often the water crept up to their feet. She scooped up some water and splashed her face.

"Okay, I'm ready," she said.

Tatiana had given them an aluminum foil survival blanket, still folded and in its wrapper. She had bought it years ago before a trip to Siberia—not the trip she had taken with Arkady but another one—and since then it had sat in her travel bag, going everywhere with her.

"I'm going to boil in that thing," Elena said.

"I know. We can't help it. But it might make a difference."

Border guards were known to use thermal scanners. Foil blankets rendered those scanners useless. If a guard ran his scanner over Arkady's car, it would not detect Elena inside as long as she was wrapped in the blanket. It wouldn't necessarily prevent a dog from finding her, and it certainly wouldn't be of any use if they had Arkady open the trunk. So the blanket was something, and something was better than nothing.

She kissed him, took the blanket from its wrapper, shook it out, and wrapped it around herself as though she were a just-finished marathon runner with a medal and aching legs.

"Ready?" Arkady asked. He handed her the water bottle.

She nodded. "Ready as I'll ever be."

He opened the trunk. She got in and curled herself up to fit the space. Arkady helped her adjust the blanket so that every part of her was covered.

"Okay," she said.

She didn't ask for reassurance, and he didn't give her any. It would work or it wouldn't.

He shut the trunk and backed the car off the road and onto the highway.

Five miles from the border, the traffic began to thicken. Arkady saw family cars and minibuses piled high with belongings. He knew that many of them were Crimean Tatars fleeing before the backlash really hit. These were the ones who hadn't left in 2014 when the Russians had first come south to Crimea, so for them to go now was a sign of how serious they felt things would become. The news had reported that it was a Tatar—and not just any Tatar but Uzeir Osmanov's daughter—who had assassinated Konstantin Novak.

As they approached the border, fences and cordoned-off lanes appeared. Arkady slowed and slowed again. A young man with glasses held up a hand and looked in through the window.

"You need special fast passage through here?" he asked.

"Who are you?"

"A facilitator."

A parasite, more likely, Arkady thought. People like these sprung up like weeds at the borders. They claimed to grease the wheels, and perhaps they did, but they also added complications where they didn't need to. They took money for their services and paid a good proportion of it to the guards for allowing them to operate there. Arkady didn't know what kind of clout this "facilitator" might have, and he didn't want to entangle himself in something unnecessary.

"I'm fine."

"It'll take you longer."

"I'm not in a hurry."

"Suit yourself."

"I will."

The man rolled his tongue into his cheek and mimed something obscene. Arkady thought about running over his foot.

A guard beckoned him forward, peered in through the window, clocked that he was alone, and directed him down a lane to the left. Arkady noticed that the Tatar cars and minibuses were being siphoned off to the right. Would they be questioned more or less than him? Would the border guards see them as easier targets for bribery? He didn't know, and he put it from his mind. He was Gennady, a photographer, traveling alone. That was who he had to be for the next few minutes at least.

Another guard directed him to a large parking lot. The man had a baton in one hand and a gun on his belt. Two soldiers in fatigues cradled machine guns and watched in unsmiling silence. The guard gestured for Arkady to wind down his window and pointed to a hut. "Passport control. Leave the car open."

Arkady patted his pocket to check he had Gennady's passport, even though he must have checked two dozen times since they'd left Sevastopol. He got out of the car feeling as though this were all happening to someone else. He needed to focus. Putting one foot in front of the other, he reached the hut and the illusion disappeared.

There was a long line inside. Of four available desks, only two were manned. Arkady counted the number of people in front of him and guessed how long it would be before it was his turn.

He could see the car outside. The guard who had directed him was now dealing with someone else. The soldiers were looking on. Arkady resolved not to look at the car anymore. If someone came to search it while he was in here, what could he do? Nothing.

The room was hot and airless. Arkady felt sweat trickle down the side of his face. He wiped it away and hoped it would be seen as a reaction to heat rather than nerves, if it was seen at all.

"You."

A border officer had opened up one of the windows and beckoned Arkady forward. He handed his passport over, open to the photograph page. The man examined it, looked at Arkady, examined the photo again, looked at Arkady again. Arkady felt himself biting back the desire to make some cheap and crass joke about passport photos. The officer didn't look the type to find it funny. Arkady wondered how much of life he'd find funny if he was stuck in a prefab passport hut seven days a week.

"Name?" said the guard.

"Gennady Artyomovich Nikitin."

"Date of birth?"

"June 12, 1964."

"Occupation?"

"Photographer."

"What kind of photographer?"

"News, mainly."

"Who do you work for?"

"I'm freelance. *Izvestia, Rossiyskaya Gazeta, Argumenty i Fakty*, lots of others." This was true in as far as it went, Gennady had worked for all of them, but more importantly they were all well-known and broadly pro-government newspapers that might help convince a border guard that Gennady was a faithful servant of the state rather than a troublemaker.

"Why are you going to Ukraine?"

"To work on a story there."

"What kind of story?"

"Fortieth anniversary of the *Mother Motherland* statue." Another nod to officialdom, this time with a garnish of imperial glory.

The guard nodded, closed Arkady's passport, and started to hand it back to him.

"Star sign?" he said suddenly.

"Excuse me?"

"What's your star sign?"

"Gemini."

The man nodded. Arkady took the passport from his hand and walked out of the hut. The breeze, slight as it was, felt delicious.

Asking someone their star sign was an old investigator's trick, and he had been ready for it. It was an easy and almost foolproof way to see if someone was who their documents proclaimed them to be. People using fake IDs would memorize their fake names and dates of birth, but they rarely remembered to find out what their fake zodiac sign was.

He got back into the car. Signs pointed him forward, around a long curve, and through a slalom of pylons. Another hut smaller than the one he had just been in seemed empty, and Arkady drove on without waiting to see whether he should have stopped.

There was another line up ahead. He rolled to a stop.

CUSTOMS, said the sign. YOUR VEHICLE MAY BE SEARCHED.

34

He waited in line for three hours. He didn't dare say a word to Elena, and her silence unnerved him. She could have become overheated in the blanket and be unconscious or dead. He told himself not to be ridiculous.

The line inched forward, one car at a time. Brake lights flared, engines coughed. Open doors hinged on cars like wings on an insect. Arkady watched as nervous passengers were taken from their cars into a hut to be questioned. Arkady's mouth was dry and his water bottle was empty. He picked at his chips, making him even more thirsty.

He inched the car to the front of the line.

A guard in olive green approached. "Pull over, turn your engine off, and get out of the car."

He did so.

"Passport."

No point in saying that he'd already shown his passport.

"Occupation?"

"Photographer."

"Where are your cameras?"

"They were stolen in Sevastopol."

"Stolen?"

"Yes."

"I was covering a Tatar protest. They knocked me to the ground and took my equipment."

"Who did?"

"Who did what?"

"Who took your equipment?"

"The protesters."

"Not the police?"

"No. The protesters. The Tatars," Arkady said.

"What do you expect? Filthy thieving bastards. What kind of cameras?"

"Two Nikons and a Leica," he improvised. "The Leica was my father's. I have some more in Kyiv."

"Step aside, please."

A handler approached with a German shepherd straining on its leash. The dog poked its nose inside the driver's door. The first guard who had questioned Arkady picked up a scanner from the table next to him, turned it on, and began to run it over the car. It shrieked as he passed it over the hood, but that was only to be expected. The engine was hot.

The dog leapt up onto the car seats and snuffled around.

Arkady had his bag of barbecue chips in his hand. He looked inside. There were three chips left, and his hands were sticky with grease and salt.

The guard was running the scanner along the passenger

side now. Arkady moved as unobtrusively as he dared to the rear of the car.

In the hut, a phone began to ring.

The guard reached the trunk. This was it. If the aluminum blanket didn't work, then it would all be over in the next few seconds.

The phone continued to ring.

The guard ran the scanner along the top of the trunk. Nothing. No electronic shriek, no demand to open the trunk. Silence.

Down the sides and along the back. Still nothing.

Now came the German shepherd.

Arkady had to time it just right, and he had to make it look natural.

He let the packet of chips slip from his fingers. The dog's head darted toward it as Arkady had hoped it would. He slowly bent to retrieve the packet and, just as he had hoped, the dog stuck his nose inside.

The dog sniffed around the rear of the car. Arkady hoped that the scent of onion, garlic, and tomato had overwhelmed all other scents in the dog's impressive olfactory system.

The dog sniffed, looked at its handler, sniffed again, looked at Arkady. Somehow, Arkady felt, it was even more capricious to have his fate decided by a dog than by an electronic scanner.

The German shepherd turned away and headed back toward the hut.

"You are now free to leave the Russian Federation," the guard said.

It was a short distance across no-man's-land to the Ukraine side of the border. The Ukrainian flag, blue as the sky and yellow as the fields, fluttered over the huts ahead. Arkady drove up and a young guard looked at his passport.

"Did you have a good one?" he asked.

"A good what?"

"Party." He pointed to Arkady's passport where a birth date was listed. "You were fifty-four last week, correct?"

"Yes," Arkady laughed. "It must have been a good one if I can't remember it."

The man stamped his passport and handed it back. "Welcome to Ukraine."

The gate swung up and Arkady drove through. He slipped "1944" into the CD player, turned up the volume, and pressed PLAY so Elena would know they had made it.

EPILOGUE

Arkady was used to February bringing the kind of cold that sliced through layers of clothing. It was the darkness that got him—that and the knowledge that there were still months to go until summer.

He didn't have to be here, of course. He could have taken his pension and retired to a warmer climate. But he knew he would never be able to adjust to a life outside of Moscow. He could leave, and often did, but he always came back.

Dr. Pavlova had gotten him on two courses, one of medication and the other of physiotherapy, and between the two they seemed to be keeping the worst at bay. "It's management," she'd said, "not a cure."

It was easier to accept when he thought about it like that. At least every day he was here at Petrovka was another small annoyance for Zurin, which in itself almost made the job worthwhile.

Zhenya had texted earlier: You okay? He did it every time Arkady went on a night shift, and his concern meant more to Arkady than he knew how to say. He remembered the furrows of concentration on Zhenya's brow when he'd first told him about the diagnosis.

"No, Zhenya," he'd said.

"No Zhenya what?"

"No, this isn't a chess problem with a solution."

"I know."

"Do me a favor, though? Don't go easy with me on the chessboard."

"Are you kidding? I'd never do that." That was the best re-assurance Arkady could have asked for.

Arkady knew that Elena wanted to come back to Moscow, but it was impossible. It wasn't safe for her—not under the current regime. Her work with the Tatars was best continued in Kyiv, where she'd be further from Putin's reach. Arkady had stayed with her for a while after they'd escaped Crimea, but eventually he came back. They were out of sync with each other perhaps because of their difference in years. She along with others of her generation were citizens of a different world.

As for Tatiana, she was still in Kyiv, reporting on Russia's invasion in and around Ukraine. They spoke once or twice a week, and, as usual, he worried about her.

ACKNOWLEDGMENTS

As usual, there are too many people to thank for all the help they have given me in the writing of this novel. Even as the COVID-19 epidemic raged, my dedicated agent, Andrew Nurnberg, flew all the way from London to California to go over the manuscript with me, pointing out any Russian mistakes I had made. Unable to go to Ukraine, I am grateful to Harry Snyder and Diana Schmidt for grounding me in the beautiful city of Kyiv, Ukraine. I am indebted to my editor, Sean Manning, for his insightful edits, his ideas, and for his patience.

It is my friend Dr. Ken Sack who first told me I had Parkinson's disease and explained to me how he knew. I learned more as the disease progressed over the next twenty years from my caring and brilliant doctor, Jill Ostrem.

Finally, I couldn't have written this book without the support of my family: Nell and Nelson Branco; Luisa Smith, who first read the manuscript and gave me valuable advice; her husband, Don Sanders; my son, Sam Smith; and of course my wife, Em.

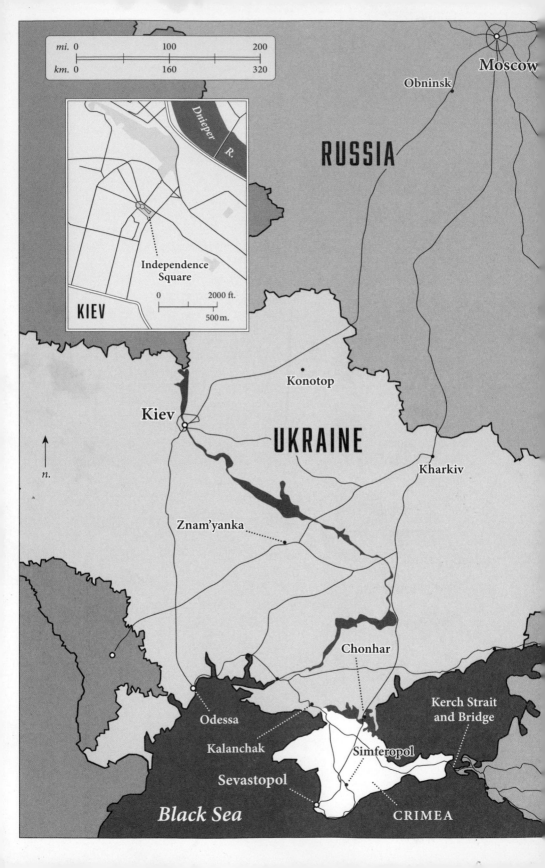